Embracing the Forgotten

A Novel

by

Ethan McGrane

Supernatural Fiction

DEDICATIONS

For Don,
You were the one who encouraged me to
pursue writing.

For My Grandmother,
For whom I have to publish all my work,
though she'll never get to read it.

**For everyone who has, or ever will read one
of my books,**
Without you, none of this would mean
anything.

"Magic lockets, past lives, demons... I didn't believe in any of that before I bought this house."

-Emma Green

Chapter 1

Shadows of Solitude

"Come on, Emmy." Not this again. "The girls love it when you're out here… so does Liam," Gerald, my brother, continues to plea.

"I know, I know. I love seeing them, too. But…" *But what, Emma? You've been making excuses your whole life. You should have a shortlist of them by now.*

Before I can say my canned, half-hearted excuse as to why I can't occupy his guest bedroom for the Labor Day weekend, I hear a whine that would make Old Scratch squeal with delight. Steel beams, stationary for the better part of a century, refuse to hold the roof of the apartment building across the street for a moment more.

The roof begins its descent through the lives of people I've passingly spied on for the last five years. My phone falls to my hip. I have to tighten my shaking hand to keep from dropping it. I watch the roof pass through the eighth floor, where the old man drinks the night away on the fire escape. He was inside for his third bathroom trip and fifth beer. I take a few unsteady steps backward as the roof descends through the sixth floor, where the single mother does the dishes as her children are in the living room enjoying their nightly video games. My mouth dries, and my upper lip curls back. So many… washed away.

I place the back of my trembling hand on the bridge of my nose and twist my body away from the window as the freefalling roof approaches the second floor. Mandy lives in *217*, a one-bedroom apartment. My best friend, who keeps me out of my shell, has had her life compacted into the subfloors.

Thirty seconds stretched into a lifetime until the impact caused the vase containing the purple hyacinths and daffodils Mandy gave me at the office today to fall. Flowers flounce in a pool of water and glass shards. I hadn't remembered Ma's birthday until Mandy gave me the flowers. After only three years of her absence, I forgot how significant August 6th was for the first three decades of my life.

After the initial shock fades, Gerald asks if I'm alright. I don't know. I don't think I am. It's easier for me to end the call than figure it out.

***

I can't move. I'm frozen to my chair, head in hands. It's almost noon, two days later. The light in my apartment still feels gray even though raw sunlight pierces the windows. The TV is off, and the clock ticks on. Silence has befallen the entire block.

Outside, a dog barks. The rescue crew found another one. Is this one alive? Is it Mandy? Do I get my best friend back after two days of mourning? If not, add them to the list of the last two-hundred and seventeen bodies they've pulled out of the pile. Only thirty-two residents have been accounted for. They have their lives, but they've lost everything they can measure.

My cell phone is dead, sitting on the kitchen table before me. The LAN line is off the hook, dangling by its curly cord. I'm exactly as I want to be right now, unreachable. I emailed all my contacts yesterday morning, letting them know I was unharmed and would be inaccessible for a few days. I don't think I'm fine. Fine people don't spend thirty-seven hours sitting at their kitchen table, watching emergency workers pull bodies out of the rubble, waiting for a shock of curly blonde hair so they can run downstairs and cross the street to identify their best friend's remains.

***

I can't stand my apartment anymore. If Mandy is still alive, it would be a miracle. I would need to attend church for the first time in my life and give all I have to the have-nots. If my apartment existed within a vacuum with no evidence of other humans, a vessel on a lonely sea, maybe I could stay. If I stay here, I only have reminders about what happened two nights ago.

I'm going to do what I always do. I will surrender all control and familiarity, and go into the unknown. I'll further complicate my crisis to distract myself from sadness. When my father died, I moved out of the house. When my mother died, I moved to Boston. Mandy's dead. Where do I go now? I pack five days' worth of clothes and some other essentials and throw them in the trunk of my 2016 BMW M5.

Once I'm on the highway, I can lean on the accelerator. The city's bustling streets blur past me as I flee the suffocating grasp of South Boston. Every mile I put between myself and the memories haunting those corridors brings a renewed sense of freedom. The weight of grief and isolation lifts from my shoulders, replaced by possibility, until the radio host said the new numbers from the search and rescue squad. There is no word on survivors, yet only twenty-one residents remain unaccounted for. My gut twists as I realize I witnessed two hundred and sixty-eight people die in less than a minute.

I can't cope with catastrophe. I'll go somewhere none

of this will be able to hurt me.

When I first fled, I intended to go to Groton and see the 'wicked renovatin'' Gerald did to his guest room. But on the Northern Expressway, instead of exiting west on I-95 to cut across to Route 3, I fled east. I'm sorry. I'm sure those renovations are great, but I don't think I can be around anyone now or ever again.

Now, navigating the winding roads leading me further north, the world outside my car transforms. Suburbs give way to rolling hills and open meadows. The cacophony of city life fades into forests. Nature's song strums along my hair, pouring in through the open window. Something is calling to me from down the road, promising solace.

***

The timeless charm of South Thornbrook.

Fate had me stop for gas in this small town. A farmhouse, whispered about in hushed conversations, becomes my beacon of hope. The town's locals speak of its abandoned state, a desolate dwelling lingering on the market for far too long. This could be the enchanting enclave to find respite from the scars haunting my weary soul.

Curiosity takes hold, and I set out to uncover the secrets within those weathered walls. I seize the opportunity to claim this forgotten farmhouse as my own. It will be my symbol of renewal, my chance to rebuild myself. With a stroke of a pen and exchange of keys, I have purchased my sanctuary.

Something within this house wants me here. I'll oblige.

Chapter 2

Decades of Dereliction

Stepping across the threshold, I feel a surge of anticipation. The house seems to hold its breath as if aware of its long-concealed secrets. Time has etched its mark upon the interior walls. Each crack and crevice whispers tales of forgotten history. Scant wallpaper remains on the walls, and most rests on the floor. A few swaths simply peel down from the ceiling. I knew this place would be derelict. The agent I purchased this house through said it's sat unused for most of the last decade.

There's a musk hanging in the air. The atmosphere is stale. I've left footsteps in the dust coating every flat surface. I should get some air circulating in here. I walk into the room on my left. There's a fireplace on the far wall. Dust covers are strewn on the floor, but no furniture is in sight. As I draw the drapes back from the glass panes, they unravel and fall from the curtain rod. The paint is peeling from the window sill, and time has warped the frame to where it is difficult to open. With some gentle pressure and a few tender pleas, the window swings outward.

This house may have been for sale for the last seven

years, but I think it's been empty for much longer. I have difficulty believing anyone occupied this house within the twenty-first century. My mind is weighed down by fog. I need to continue exploring my sanctuary.

The fireplace is filthy. I would likely burn the whole place down if I used it. Past the fireplace, toward the rear of the house, there's another room. The walls are composed of bookcases, and an old desk dominates the middle of the room. Nothing but dust stands upon the shelves. The drawers are missing from the desk.

There is a tight passage leading under the stairs to the main hall. The back door is boarded from the outside. A hammer and crowbar have been added to my mental shopping list the next time I go into South Thornbrook. Still, through the boards, the grass blanketing the landscape between the house and the rocky coast is breathtaking.

Facing the front of the house, there is a door directly on my left. I open it, and it reveals a staircase leading into pure darkness. A basement and two floors? The agent was crazy to sell me this house for only seventy-eight thousand dollars. I can fix this place while I fix myself, and when I'm done, the house will be worth at least half a million dollars.

I don't quite dare to enter the basement yet. I better make sure the rest of the house isn't haunted first. What are the odds of only the basement being haunted? I close the door, which grinds against its frame, and check the next door. This door is sloped at the top right-hand corner to fit under the stairs. It opens into a half bathroom containing only a toilet and a sink.

I turn right after returning to the foyer. A large table spans the length of this room. There are no chairs in sight. I have an urge to open the windows in this dining room, but something compels me to leave them be. Why should I not be able to part the drapes adorning the windows of my own house? Why should I not be able to see through to the outside? I push through the primordial hesitation retching to the surface of my spirit, and move toward the window on the north side of the room.

Electricity pulses through my arm when my hand touches the tattered curtain. My hand locks shut around the fabric. Is this for real, or is my fear causing a psychosomatic response? I have no reason to be afraid. There is no logic behind this. I jerk my arm to the right, and the curtain rod pulls from the screws securing it to the wall. With a clamor, it falls to the floor, and a sprinkling of plaster dust floats lightly toward the floor in contrast to the raucous display of the brass fixture.

I look through the window out into the field. There's nothing there, so I look past the grass toward the line of evergreen trees. Past the forest's edge, it is black, utterly devoid of light. Maybe I don't know the ways of the world, but in the deciduous forests of oaks and maples bordering my childhood home, the canopy never stole the light from the forest floor.

I need to keep moving through the house. Every time I stop, I feel something breathe into my ear. Something wants me to do something, and when I do nothing, it becomes impatient. I turn right and again walk to the back of the house. Logically, the room adjacent to the dining room should be the kitchen, and this house has a logical layout. The kitchen seems uncharacteristically lovely to be in a place I estimate to have sat empty for two decades.

The sink is brushed steel, so bright it almost looks to be made of the sunlight penetrating the small window directly above it. It may be higher quality than the sink in my luxury apartment in South Boston. The oven looks dated but in good shape. The white enamel of the surface has scuffed in some places, exposing the bare steel underneath, but if I had the desire to fry an egg, I could easily accomplish that with the unit. To my surprise, there is a dishwasher and a refrigerator that look ten years old. Whoever lived here last skimped on everything except the kitchen.

Countertops line the north and east sides of the kitchen, and a table sits alone at the southwest corner. The drawers missing from the study's desk are stacked atop this table, which also has no chairs. Were the previous owners really so attached to their seating arrangements?

Stacks of old, yellow-edged papers are sitting next to the drawers. They all look like bills when I shuffle through them. I can flip through these bills to simplify the process when I want to set up the internet or another utility. For now, I have to keep exploring.

I think I've seen everything there is to see on the first floor, so I climb the stairs to the second floor. Where there was a hallway on the first floor, there is a walkway on the second. The majority of the space, though, is cut out by the stairway. There are windows at both ends of the hallway, but it feels unnaturally dark and oppressive here on the second level. I flip the light switch, but the light does not ignite. I look up. The socket has a bulb, but I can't tell if it's burned out or the power is off.

I open the door immediately next to me. The whole bathroom is illuminated once my phone's flashlight turns on. I flip the light switch, and this one stays off too. If I go into the next room and the light is off, three for three means the power is off. I walk across the hall and open the door. This room is blindingly bright compared to the rest of the house. There is no obscuring upon the window. I try the light switch anyway, and it does not turn on either.

I go downstairs, and with my phone flashlight at the ready, I open the door to the basement and descend the stone stairs. The small windows are covered in dust and grime to where they don't let in any worthwhile amount of light. It is off-puttingly damp down here. I shine the flashlight to my right. There is a shelf standing in the corner. This basement is cavernous, dungeonlike. I don't like being down here. The battery percentage on the upper right corner of my phone screen ticks away. I walk around, making my way to the back of the basement. I pass a few lights along the way, but as I pull their cords, no illumination expels the darkness of this subterranean chamber.

I find my way to a laundry station under the kitchen at the northeast corner of the house. The washer and dryer look old but newer than most things in this house. I turn right, and there is a little nook behind the stairs. The water heater and well are tucked away in this corner.

I had expected to find the circuit breaker by now but have yet to see it in my search. Did I miss it upstairs?

I walk along the stairs back to their base. Maybe I've seen too many movies, but I feel as though something is in the corners of this basement, waiting for the moment my phone, and thus flashlight, dies.

Silly me, I must have walked right by the breaker. It's on the westernmost wall of the basement, right at the bottom of the stairs. I slide the latch to the left and gently open the door. Its rusted hinges squeal as the door swings. I'm on eggshells with this house after the incidents with the two curtains.

As I'm checking the circuits, something whispers to me from upstairs. I felt it whisper to me instead of hearing it. Maybe my mind is playing tricks on me. All of the switches are on. The only reason there wouldn't be power to the house is that there is no power from the grid. My phone vibrates as my battery drops to fifteen percent. I turn off the flashlight as I climb the stairs. I shuffle a little faster up the last few steps, feeling the fangs of imagined demons nip at my heels.

I shut the basement door and walk over to the kitchen. I wish I could sit down for the duration of this activity. My flats are not the best shoes for exploring, and my arches are long past tender. Come to think of it, I haven't seen a single chair in this house so far. I begin the arduous tedium of searching through the papers on the table next to the desk drawers.

Some of these bills have been… redacted, for lack of a better word. The first bill I find is for a credit card. The company's logo is intact, but the name underneath the logo has been whited out, along with the cardholder name, the account number, the statement date, and other information within the document. It doesn't even look like whiteout was used. Maybe it fades to be unnoticeable after a few years? It seems like the ink of any personally identifiable information evaporated off the paper. The next bill is an invoice for a truckload of gravel, then one for tree stump grinding, a cord of firewood, etc…

As I'm nearing the bottom of the pile, I find a pink piece of paper from the electric company. Their phone number is at the top of the page, right under the logo. Thank you, the previous habitant of this house, for not redacting this bill like your credit card statements.

The phone call was unexpectedly expedient. The service, however, is less. The slightly accented voice on the other side of the phone said the company would have to reinstate the account, transfer it to my name from the information I gave them, and send a technician out. When I asked them for a time estimate, they told me by ten o'clock tomorrow morning. It's only four-thirty in the evening right now.

Chapter 3

An Inaudible Whisper

I smooth back my hair as I sit down on the stairs. This is the closest thing I have to a chair in this house. Was this a mistake? I'm all alone out here. But I was trying to be alone. I don't know how I can be around people when I'm so vulnerable. I wish I could use the last seven percent of my phone battery to call Mandy. My Schroedinger friend is in limbo. I have no idea if she's alive under the rubble or not. I never saw her pulled out of the debris. If I close my eyes, can I pretend she's living it up down there in her one-bedroom apartment that's been rammed into the basement, or will I only see the building falling at the speed of tragedy through ten floors of people's lives?

I drop my head into my hands, feeling the weariness settle in my bones. A pang of hunger twists in my stomach, a reminder that a meal is overdue. I should go get something to eat. The gnawing emptiness in my belly echoes the necessity. Glancing at my recent history of neglect, I realize that the bag of chips snagged from the gas station yesterday stands as the sole entry in my meager food log. In fact, those chips marked the first inception of nourishment after a hiatus that stretched beyond mere hours — it spans a couple of long, exhausting days.

With my personality, instead of choosing what kind of restaurant I want to go to, I'm trying to figure out how to get food in a way where I can interact with as few people as possible. I could go to a restaurant, sit in the corner booth all alone, or sit at the bar and wait for one of the other patrons to drink enough to tell me they've never seen me "around these parts before." I don't know if I want to be around these people at all. I'm the strange lady who drove into town on a whim and bought the odd house on the outskirts. That's what they'll think of me. To them, I'm just the strange lady with the strange house.

Seventeen minutes tick away in silent contemplation as I spiral into the labyrinth of thoughts concerning what strangers might perceive about me and my new home. The phrase "my new home" echoes in my mind, sending a surge through my nervous system like a revitalizing current. There's an excitement, a promise lingering in the unexplored corners of my newfound sanctuary. The realization dawns that, despite the ticking minutes, I haven't seen all my new home holds within its walls yet. A sense of anticipation dances in the air, urging me to embark on the journey of discovery that awaits beyond each unopened door.

I rise from my perch and climb the stairs to the second floor. The full bathroom is on the right, and the first door on the left is a bedroom. The cracked and worn wall stretches to another door, standing alone in the corner. There used to be pictures or paintings on the wall. The wallpaper has peeled away from the nails that once held vague feelings or fond memories.

The door at the end of the hall opens into another bedroom. Somebody has swept the dust and debris into a neat pile in the middle of the room. They didn't pick it up, though, and now the pile and the rest of the room are once again covered in dust and debris. So much work needs to be done to this house. Gerald would know precisely what needs to be done. I made a mistake buying this house. Restoring it will be impossible, just like healing myself.

I pull the door shut and turn around. There's one last door I've yet to open. I turn the handle but do not feel the inner mechanism turn with it. I pull, and the door doesn't budge. I prise more, and the handle comes straight off, the jolt causing me to land flat on my back. With the state of this house, I'm surprised I am not lying in the foyer right now.

I get up, suspecting the back of my red-and-white pinstripe blouse is now gray from the dust. I look at the floor where I landed. It doesn't look like the dust was disturbed too much. The room is bright inside, artificially so. There's a light hum. I think the power is back on. As someone who's experienced the corporate world, it appears they used the "under promise and over deliver" tactic with me, for it is far from ten o'clock tomorrow morning.

The door swings open effortlessly, revealing what I deduce to be the master bedroom. Its spaciousness feels incongruent with the modest exterior of the house. My attention is immediately drawn to a substantial bedframe in the center of the room. However, the absence of a mattress leaves me wistful. I yearn for a comfortable surface to lay my head on. I shudder at the thought of another night spent cramped in my car. The prospect of restful sleep becomes increasingly appealing.

The same inaudible whisper I heard in the basement earlier calls to me again. I thought anything wanting to be found would be in this last room of the house. I turn around and walk down the hallway again. I must have missed something on the first floor, but as I step to the top of the stairs, I'm interrupted by the whisper again.

I turn around and feel the whisper when I reach the

midway point between the two bedrooms. I glance around, but nothing stands out. I roll my eyes, and then I see it: the entrance to the attic. The cord is too high, so I must jump to reach it. The pull-down stairs jerk open in a way that triggers my flight instincts, but I force myself to hold onto it and not let it slam onto the floor. Decades of dust lilted through the air, recreating the effect of a smoke machine in a 1970s UFO. I step back and cover my nose with my shirt sleeve to avoid breathing it in.

I ascend the creaking stairs, the skin on my neck prickling with each step, a sensation made more intense by this hushed atmosphere. The first sight greeting my eyes is a blank white wall, starkly contrasting the aged dereliction that defines the rest of the structure. I turn around, and despite the narrowness of this space, a sense of intimacy settles in, as if the house's very essence is concentrated here beneath the gabled roof. The dimensions may be modest, but the attic has an undeniable allure, where the past lingers in a dance of shadows and dust motes.

The floor creaks loudly with each step as I make my way to the east wall. I see scuff marks and spots where old furniture and storage vessels used to sit. Maybe a card table or other flimsy apparatus once stood here. I'm imagining pirate chests, old gramophones, a rocking chair with a doll containing the souls of murdered children, and the devil himself. But this attic is empty, which may be more frightening than anything that could occupy the space.

The view from this window is incredible. It's a round window, not much broader than I am. It overlooks the two hundred feet between the house and the ocean. The shoreline is a beautiful barrier of grey crags between the rolling green grass and lazy blue sea. I want to take a picture and send it to Mandy. She would enjoy the view. But my phone is dead. She is, too.

A shiver runs the length of my spine, pulling me from

the motionless pondering of my lost friend, causing me to turn around. The wall at the west side of the attic, which looked out of place with its flawless white paint, now has a door. I know the door wasn't there. I won't pretend I didn't see it. There's no way this door was there five minutes ago. The circuit breaker in the basement was easy to write off as a simple mistake. This door, the apparition of it, something feels sinister about it. There's something behind the door. What lies in the chamber beyond it has been whispering to me throughout the afternoon. Whispering without making a sound. I have to know what's in there, but every fiber of my body is repulsed simultaneously.

My ribs feel too tight around the trembling inflation of my lungs and the speeding of my heart. The hairs upon my body are standing up, tears preemptively well in my eyes. Don't do it, my instincts scream. But I have to know what's in the room.

Ethan McGrane

Ethan McGrane

Chapter 4

The Memory Room

I push the ghost door open. The dust suspended in the atmosphere catches the light from the window, lending the room an ethereal appearance. As I step into the chamber, a tingling sensation prickles the back of my neck. The air crackles as if the room itself holds the secrets. The room is nearly empty. The wall, its smooth white appearance, is only a facade. Back here, it's wooden frames with the gray paper backing of drywall showing through.

In the far corner is an armchair, the first chair I've seen in this house, and a small table. I can't determine what's on the table from here, so I must fight my instincts and delve deeper. It's a silver locket with a swirling floral pattern on it. A delicate chain is strewn on the surface of the table. I don't like this room, but I feel compelled to sit.

A weight lifts from my shoulders as I sink into the chair. The tension following me around the house is relieved. A shadow darts about at the corner of my eye, but I don't mind it. The door is still there. It is still open. I have nowhere to be except right here right now. I embrace the opportunity to relax for the first time today.

***

Perhaps I relaxed too much. I rub the heaviness out of my eyelids in near blackness. My mind recalls the oddity of my discovering this room. As I ponder the purpose of this room's existence, another whisper expels the racing thoughts within my mind. This whisper is angelic in sound but metallic in tone. It doesn't feel like the one that led me here. That one felt like someone else was giving me their feelings, their intuitions. No, this new whisper feels impatient, as though they've waited years for me to be sitting where I am.

It is… Memory Room

The Memory Room? I didn't come here to remember. I came here to forget. I want to forget the awful things I've witnessed, to bury the haunting memories beneath the floorboards of this old farmhouse. I yearn to be absorbed into my new life, to cocoon myself in the quaint routines of South Thornbrook, and pretend I've always been a part of this community. I want to shield myself from the shadows of the past, to craft a narrative where nothing traumatic happened to me before I purchased this house. Yet, even as I stand here, resisting the pull of the Memory Room, I can't shake the echoes of those distant experiences, lingering like whispers in the corners of my mind.

You can't forget.

I don't like this new whisper. I know I can't forget. My whole life can be replayed in painful detail. Every time I scraped my knee, every time one of the other girls pulled my hair, every time I sat alone at lunch, every time Gerald would ask me to sit in the forest between our house and his friend Ricky's house because I was no good at the game they had planned, but mom wouldn't let him leave me behind. In middle school, something happened that I can't put my finger on. It was like a flip of the off-switch, as if one day, the engineer pulled the lever to halt the blood flow to the part of my brain that made me want to talk to, interact with, or even be around other people.

I grab the locket off the table, dangling it in front of me in the air. Why was this little locket left behind? The previous owner was thorough in taking their old things. Lockets are usually significant, holding old memories and emotions. A small picture someone wanted close to their heart. Mine is the only heart here now.

The button on top of the locket causes the shell to spring open. Tonight's darkness doesn't fulfill its duty to obscure the picture within the locket. A man in a suit with a neatly groomed beard, neat right-parted hair, and oddly pale eyes smiles at me. The edges of my vision close in, and the man's eyes seem to emit light the closer the darkness of my sight strangles the peripheral.

As darkness swallows the last of my sight, a kaleidoscope of colors floods my retinas. I'm no longer in the Memory Room. Where I am now is substantially larger. The ceiling above me is composed of steel beams. The walls of smooth concrete are covered in various paintings. The sun peers between skyscrapers through the window, casting a bright, golden hue on everything. I'm not in control.

The stool creaks as I shift my weight to pick up a rag from the small table beside me. My hands, *these aren't my hands*, are covered in swatches of vibrant paint. I wipe the paint from my fingertips and the underside of my hands. I have these colors painted on the back of my hand on purpose. I'm trying to figure out which color would be best for the background of this artwork.

I hold the back of my hand up next to the easel. There's a pencil sketch on the canvas. A drawing of the same locket I'm holding in a derelict farmhouse in rural Maine. What color should I use? What color would be most appropriate for an artifact of this significance and power? Should I use purple, with blue highlights, swirling around the locket to capture the mystique, or red, with black shadowing, to give it a more sinister appearance?

I don't know enough about the locket to make a good decision. The best art should represent things as they genuinely are. The room pulses with creative energy, but I don't have the authority, the divine dictation to discern the qualities of this locket one of my patrons gave me and asked me to immortalize.

Over to the rotary phone by the door, I ask the operator to connect me with the patron, Thomas Harrison. After a brief exchange, he tells me the locket came to him through mysterious circumstances, and they don't know its past. It's a dead end, but I'm resourceful. I ask the operator for a list of antique collectors and jewelry appraisers within the city.

I hate speaking on the phone or in person, but I must put on a friendly facade. An artist can't survive without rubbing a few elbows in this city. It took four calls before one of the collectors, a New England Occult Society member, agreed to sit down with me.

"What name should I put down for your appointment?"

"Evans, Amelia Evans," I answer.

"I'll see you at twenty to noon, Ms. Evans."

I'm Amelia Evans? The painter who became famous for portraying human spirits. She found her success by illustrating spiritual concepts. One of her pieces is on the wall in my apartment in Boston.

The line goes dead, and I flip the locket open. There's an energy to it. Something ancient about this necklace. Who's the man inside? Who did the locket belong to? What were their fates? Why is the locket no longer in their family?

I sigh. Though I have a meeting tomorrow, I am far from understanding this locket. I wanted a history of this locket. Not some occultist speaking of hidden power locked away. What if the man inside the locket was an occultist?

Maybe then I'm on the right track. I go to the bathroom. I'm done with my work for now.

In the sink, the paint from the back of my hand slowly runs off with the water, swirling around the drain, a rainbow drawn into a black void of non-existence. I look up into the mirror, and Amelia's eyes meet mine. I've never looked into a mirror through someone else's eyes. There's an instinct, something telling me this is wrong. This isn't me, but it should be. Some of the features are close enough. The eyes, the same shape, but Amelia's have a spark of... brilliance? Curiosity? Ambition? There's something in the eyes looking at me through the mirror I'm not accustomed to seeing in my own.

The uncanny valley has been triggered. Fear pierces my heart. I – Amelia reaches up and runs her fingers from her jaw to her chin. Her brows furrow. Is the illusion breaking for both of us? Is my heart beating rapidly, or is hers? Why can't I breathe? I'm trying to breathe, but the rhythm is not my own. Amelia moves her hand to the back of her neck, her fingernails digging in. She turns and walks from the sink to the other side of the room. When she turns around, shadows swirl where the sink should be. She walks into the wall of shadows.

Nothingness washes over me. Everything that was no longer is as the kaleidoscope of colors returns me to the chair in the Memory Room. I don't want to move, but I fear I will be projected through time once more if I stay here. My phone is dead, the moon cannot reliably guide me down the stairs, and I would have nowhere else to go even if it could.

Take time to reflect on what you saw.

"I don't want to," I answer out loud.

You must.

I get up and walk toward the door, intending to exit the room. It's dark. Even in the dark, I can tell the door has disappeared. There is no exit from this room.

I sigh and sit down in the chair. I have so many questions about what I saw, but I have even more questions about my current captor.

I'm not important.

"I beg to differ."

Fine. I'll answer three questions about me. Past that, I'll only answer questions about what you saw.

"What are you, a genie?"

No, I'm a spirit bound to this room.

"Why were you bound here?"

To guide those who use this room.

"You're not being very elaborate in your answers. What is the purpose of this room?"

This room... those who created it and bound me here, wanted it to be a place where those who need healing can seek solace and reflect. You still have one question about me.

"Who were you before the guardian of this room?"

I was human, but I can't remember.

"Why was I called to this house? I felt you beckon from Boston."

Your past lives... your antecessors, those you were before you were yourself, have an... extensive intertwining with the locket.

"So, I used to be Amelia Evans?"

Yes, and many more. I want answers, and you may be the only person to give them to me.

"What was that shadow at the end of the vision."

Someone else is watching, someone outside my knowledge and control. Your arrival in this house has not gone unnoticed. We are not the only ones who know of the locket.

"What should I do now?"

Sleep. Sleep until the morning, and remember what the memories teach you. Just as Amelia sought an expert, so should you.

Chapter 5

My New Hometown

The sky, a canvas of pale blue, slowly reveals itself as I awaken. The landscape beneath, shrouded in darkness, lacks any discernable details. My attempt to sleep away the night's obscurity proved futile, and now, in this lingering darkness, before I can descend the stairs and find the nearest light switch, I find myself reflecting on the profound experiences of the past night. It's a peculiar moment, caught between the remnants of night and the forthcoming dawn, and I welcome the quiet introspection that accompanies it. As I sit here, the events of the previous night replay in my mind, each fragment seeking meaning in the dimly lit corridors of memory.

What do I know about this locket? The answer echoes in the chambers of my mind: very little. It rests within the confines of my house, concealed in a secret room where an irritable spirit stands as its vigilant guardian. This locket, once possessed by Amelia Evans, holds a mystique that eluded her comprehension just as it eludes mine. Amelia, an artist entwined with the whims of patrons, received the locket as part of a commission. Yet, even the patron who bestowed this curious artifact couldn't fathom its true nature. Struggling with the same ambiguity, Amelia felt handicapped in portraying the locket faithfully, compelled to unravel its secrets before capturing it on canvas.

Did Amelia, in her pursuit of understanding, unravel the mysteries of the locket? Did she bring to life the secrets concealed within its intricate design with the strokes of her brush? As I traverse the corridors of speculation, the haunting question persists: Why did I relive one of her memories? Could Amelia's essence, her soul, be entwined with the locket, whispering in inaudible tones, guiding me to this secluded room? Contemplating the intricate dance between her and the locket, I ponder whether Amelia intentionally placed it here, a guardian of its potent capabilities, deterring ordinary souls from stumbling upon its extraordinary power. The connection between Amelia and the locket, a labyrinth of uncertainty, beckons me to unlock the secrets that linger in the shadows of her artistic endeavors.

Within the confines of this Memory Room, can I traverse the landscapes of my past? With the gentle touch of the locket, can I revisit the cherished moments, the tender embrace of my mother, the laughter shared with Mandy, the triumphant steps towards a college diploma? Perhaps the locket will let me relive experiencing my favorite bands live for the first time. Why tether my journey solely to the recollections of others? Unless this room harbors a deliberate intent, orchestrating a revelation meant solely for my understanding. The locket may be a conductor of time, poised to unveil the threads binding me to history.

The landscape is bathed in a gentle orange hue. I unfurl myself from the chair, relishing a brief stretch that eases the knots in my back, remnants of an uncomfortable night spent sitting. Despite the lingering dimness within the house, the soft morning light beckons me to descend the ladder to the second floor. With a deft motion, I fold the stairs back into the ceiling, bridging the realms between my home and the lair of shadows above.

My stomach emits an audible protest as I descend to the ground floor. Surveying the vacant expanse of my house, a stark reminder of its emptiness, I appreciate the newly restored electricity by flipping one of the light switches on and off. However, the promise of illumination does little to quell the persistent growl from my stomach. Exploring the kitchen cabinets reveals a barrenness mirroring the rest of the house—I lack both sustenance and the means to prepare a meal. Even if provisions were within reach, the absence of cooking implements would render them as inert as the vacant spaces around me.

A shopping spree is undoubtedly on the horizon. Fiscal responsibility has been a constant companion throughout my life, manifesting in a knack for saving money. In fact, my financial prudence became so pronounced that I found it necessary to open a second bank account when the first one approached the FDIC insurance limit. The notion of opening a third account lingered on the horizon, a plan that, until recently, seemed prudent. However, the acquisition of this house has effectively reallocated those funds. In the grand scheme of renovations and restorations, possessing such a substantial sum will undoubtedly serve as a bulwark against the challenges awaiting me. The lifelong investment in savings is poised to save me from the pitfalls of restorative real estate and the metaphorical blood, sweat, and tears that come with the ambitious endeavor of refurbishing this house.

As I leave the farmhouse, the morning sun greets me with its warm embrace. This is my first excursion into town since buying the house. Excitement mingles with apprehension as I set out from my newfound sanctuary. I'm excited about acquiring the bare necessities to make my life comfortable, but I'm apprehensive about being around people. South Thornbrook felt quaint and welcoming the last time I was there. Maybe the setting reflects the people's spirit, and they will be just as welcoming as the multi-colored buildings on the town's main strip.

Rumbling hunger pangs guide me into the welcoming glow of *Danny's Diner.* The tantalizing aroma of comfort food hangs over the parking lot. Hopefully, this is a suitable venue for a brief respite. I check my emails on my partially charged phone while I wait for my food.

The stench of cigarettes greets me as I walk in. There is a man in the corner, wearing a suit that's color sits somewhere between blue and lavender. His ensemble and demeanor lend him a strange air, as though he is a movie character brought to life from a period piece about a jazz musician in 1950s Mississippi. He ashes his cigarette into a coffee mug resting on the inner edge of the bar. This old-time diner is intriguing, like stepping sixty years into the past. Then again, I stepped seventy years into the past by looking at a piece of jewelry in my attic. Still, I don't smoke and never have, so I sit at the booth in the corner opposite the restaurant from the well-dressed man.

Before my email loads, a bubbly, middle-aged waitress with curly hair walks over to my table and hands me a menu.

"Well, hey there!" she says, uncomfortably loud. "I'm Tiffany. Everyone calls me 'Tiff,' though. Anyway, you just passin' through? Haven't seen you in here before."

Words escape me. I think I'm still trying to respond to her name when my mind is trying to respond to my residence status. Luckily, I don't have to answer. The well-dressed man in the corner calls over.

"She's the one who bought the Oak Cove House." His accent is unexpectedly foreign, somewhere around French. His voice surprises me so much that I don't think about how he knows me. I suppose word spreads fast in a town like this. I must not have hidden the confusion well because he takes the liberty of introducing himself.

"I'm Cedric. Didn't mean to intrude."

"I'm Emma," I answer. It's all I can get out before Tiff starts again.

"Well, that house is a real fixer-upper. But I hope we see you here more, Emma. Can I start you off with some coffee?"

"Sure, thanks."

Tiff tops off the mug she sat down with the menu. I say "no thanks" when she asks if I want cream or sugar.

"Can I get you something to eat? I doubt that old house has a working kitchen."

"The kitchen is surprisingly nice, actually. But I don't have any food at the house."

"Well, we've got plenty of food here."

"I'll go with one egg, over easy, two pieces of turkey bacon, crispy, and some home fries."

"Okey Dokey. You're in luck today. The old man himself is in the kitchen. I'll have Danny get started on that for you."

"Thanks."

I look down at my phone, intending to go back to checking my emails. But Cedric slides onto the bench across the table from me.

"It's a special house you bought. Take care of it."

My thoughts swirl like a tempest. Images flooded my mind, each vying for attention, leaving me incapable of conjuring coherent words. In the whirlwind of mental snapshots, I grapple to articulate my feelings to Cedric before the moment slips away like sand through clasped fingers. The urgency to share, to anchor these ephemeral thoughts in conversation, became a race against time as I struggled to regain control over the maelstrom within. Cedric departed, and with him, the loss of an opportunity to articulate what had consumed my mind for the last thirteen hours.

I don't know how special the house is. I know it has a room hidden away in the attic with a locket, and looking into the locket lets you see a memory from a dead painter. Amelia was looking for someone who may know the history of the locket. Maybe I need to take the Guardian's advice and seek out an expert on the house. Find the people who occupied the house before me and ask them about the room and locket. I need answers, but finding them would make it the first time in my life I got answers.

When Tiff returns to drop off my breakfast, I ask her if there's a town historian who has been around for a while and knows the area. She scrunches her face exaggeratedly, furrowing her brows and making an audible "hmmmm…" She's even loud when she has nothing to say.

Her eyes light up with excitement as she tells me about an elderly gentleman named Henry. He's spent his whole life in this town. His head is a treasure trove of stories and memories. With eagerness, I inquire where I may find him, and Tiff takes a few moments to draw a small map on a napkin. From here, to the main road, a right after a tax accountant, two more rights, a left, and all the way down a dead-end street will take me to his quaint cottage on the outskirts of town.

Breakfast was incredible, the best I've had in a while. After it was done, I parked in a small lot off the main street near some furniture stores I saw. I wandered down the sidewalk, past charming shops and colorful facades. I spotted a cozy antique store, its window displays beckoning me inside. As I browsed the collection, I couldn't help but feel a sense of nostalgia for the farmhouse's history, longing to fill it with pieces that would complement its rustic charm.

After finding a few vintage treasures and securing a delivery time later this afternoon, I decided to explore further and sought a hardware store to stock up on tools. The helpful store owner guided me through the aisles, offering advice and anecdotes about renovating old houses. I smiled, grateful for the warm hospitality of this close-knit community. I bought a mattress and a box spring, too. The frame in the master bedroom looked about queen-sized.

I parked my car in front of the last stop for today, a small cottage surrounded by pine trees near the coast. Upon stepping on Henry's porch, the door opened.

"You must be the young lady who bought the Oak Cove House. Please, come in."

Chapter 6

This Old Man

I find profound respect in the presence of this keeper of history. His warm smile greeted me, inviting me into his snug living room. We settled amid a treasure trove of photographs and relics, remnants of past eras. The walls here are a scrapbook adorned with carefully preserved newspaper articles chronicling every noteworthy aspect of this quaint town's history. Each page is a testament to the rich tapestry woven by time, whispered tales of moments that have shaped the collective narrative of this community.

Henry wove a captivating narrative of South Thornbrook's bygone days, skillfully intertwining the threads of generational stories into a rich tapestry of the town's history. As he spoke, he sparingly mentioned the farmhouse as a bastion of the MacLeod family, its walls now standing as silent witnesses, guarding the secrets of those who have gone.

I sat for hours, captivated by Henry's storytelling, my attention fully absorbed in South Thornbrook's history. His infectious passion for preserving the past created an intimate connection, and the once-unfamiliar town now felt like a place I could call home.

Henry's narratives spanned the spectrum of emotion, from riveting tales of a corrupt 1950s politician's mysterious murder to poignant stories of a tragic boating accident that stole away his high school sweetheart and friends just days after graduation. Amidst the gravity of these accounts, his oddly joyful retelling of the animal shelter's opening struck a unique chord, even as I observed no evidence of pets around. As painted by Henry, the varied tapestry of South Thornbrook's history was as intricate as life itself.

Upon direct inquiry about the farmhouse's previous owner, Henry shared that the original family, who built the house, had seemingly abandoned it in the early 1980s. Subsequently, a wealthy lawyer from Washington, DC, became its new owner, utilizing it as a vacation home. The lawyer's daughter even celebrated her wedding in the backyard, adding a touch of familial joy to the property's history. However, the lawyer disappeared one day, leaving the house empty, even after the state seized it and its eventual sale in 2015. The identity of the subsequent owner remained shrouded in mystery, as no one in town ever saw them, extending a shadow over the property.

I ask Henry about Amelia Evans, if she was ever associated with the house.

"The artist? No, I never heard anything about her staying at the house. A famous painter staying in town would have drawn attention. I'm certain I would have heard about it."

"I found something in the house that used to belong to her," I say.

"A painting? It wouldn't be surprising. The lawyer had good taste and quite a bit of money."

"No, something smaller, a piece of jewelry."

"How do you know it belonged to Amelia Evans?"

That's a good question. I hadn't thought of how to explain that without sounding crazy. So I had to lie.

"There was a shadowbox tucked away in the corner of the attic. It was a necklace. The plaque said it was Amelia Evans's."

"It was probably just a collectible, then," Henry says.

Silence dominates the room for the next minute. Henry shuffles through some newspapers, not settling on any one of them long enough to discern their content, not once readjusting his glasses.

He glances at his watch, which he wore with the face on the palm side of his wrist, something common among veterans. Looking back at me, he sighs and says, "I'm sorry to cut our visit short. Going through this old stuff again has been a delight, and I'm glad the Oak Cove House is in your hands. You seem resourceful, and I'm sure you'll have it fixed up in no time. I forgot I have a doctor's appointment, and I'm afraid I'm going to be late for it."

I thank him for his time and all the knowledge he had shared with me. I return to the farmhouse with a heart full of gratitude and a mind filled with yet another person's memories. One day, maybe not Henry, but the town's next Henry will be able to tell of my stories within its walls.

I was late for an appointment, too. When I pulled into my driveway, I was greeted not with the sight of a house alone amongst the grassy hills but by the headlights of a box truck. We both had to brake hard, and the truck reversed back to my home as I followed in.

The same delivery driver works for all the stores on Main Street. He and his partner move the furniture, primarily chairs, into the house. They put those in the living room, out of the way, and then they brought my mattress and box spring up to the master bedroom, struggling around the sharp turn at the top of the stairs. I thought one of them would fall through the railing a couple of times, but they got the cargo onto the frame in the bedroom, right where I wanted it.

Of course, now with furniture in the house, I realized

all the other stuff I forgot to buy, bed sheets and pillows chief among them, but I can improvise for tonight. At least I have more now than I started today with. Tomorrow I'll have to go grocery shopping. Today's breakfast at Danny's should tide me over until then.

There's a lot of work yet to be done, but now I can live with a degree of comfort while I continue to improve.

Chapter 7

Ishtar's Priestess

It isn't the discomfort from the polyester surface of the mattress clinging to my skin, nor the lack of support from the folded bath towel I'm trying to use as a pillow, nor the slight crackle of the air conditioner on the window keeping me awake.

Above my head lies the cause of my restlessness — the Memory Room, its allure calling out to me ceaselessly. Sleep eludes me as the pull of that hidden space lingers in my thoughts. I've skillfully evaded its grasp throughout the day, resisting the urge to enter. However, the growing realization that I've distanced myself for too long from the secrets it holds begins to gnaw at my curiosity.

I've no evidence of God. If he's out there, does he know of this Memory Room my bare feet pad along the grimy hardwood floors toward? If he knows of it, does he condone its existence and my use?

Before I complete my contemplation of the universe's administrator and their potential oversights, the locket rests cool against my palm, its ornate design captivating me with its intricate beauty. With a deep breath, I close my eyes. I need this moment to slow my breathing and settle my heart. The Guardian surprised me by remaining silent. I click the locket open and likewise open my eyes.

The transit was less jarring this time. I found myself standing on unfamiliar ground beneath a sky ablaze with the hues of dawn. The air is alive with the scents of sand and incense, and the distant sound of a bustling city reaches my ears. I look down, smoothing wrinkles and brushing dust off my flowing garments of rich colors and intricate patterns. I feel the cool touch of beads against my skin, a necklace of significance and power.

Before me stands the grand ziggurat, a colossal monument to the gods. It juts into the sky, a testament to human devotion to their celestial connections. I begin ascending the steps, my heart racing and my breath shallow. With each step, I feel the energy of ages past surging through me, my soul resonating with the echoes of forgotten rituals.

The view is breathtaking at the summit—a sprawling cityscape stretches as far as the eye can see, its streets bustling with life. The sounds of merchants trading goods, children playing in the streets, and the aroma of food fill the air. I marvel at the organized chaos, feeling the pulse of a civilization on the brink of greatness. I've seen sketches of this in my old school textbooks. This is one of the first cities humans built. This is Eridu, in ancient Sumeria.

Though I'm not in control, the following action feels natural. I outstretch my arms, feeling the sun warm my swarthy skin. The mind I occupy, she thinks in a different language than I do, but I can understand her thoughts nonetheless. *The sun, thank the gods for giving us the sun.*

Turning around, facing the temple atop the ziggurat instead of the city below, I begin walking. A group of men dressed in gowns nearly as regal as mine start walking toward me. They speak loud enough to hear but not loud enough to be intelligible. Before our trajectories collide, the scene warps.

With the same stride, I wander through the city's labyrinthine alleyways. Temples dedicated to various deities stand tall, adorned with vibrant murals depicting scenes from myths and legends. The bustling marketplace was a tapestry of colors, and noises were hard to discern from arguments or laughter ringing out.

I find a serene oasis in a quiet courtyard, a lush garden filled with exotic flora. A pond reflects the image of a temple dedicated to Ishtar, the goddess of love and fertility, my goddess. I've been devoted to Ishtar since I was old enough to think. Her name and mine are the same, for without her, I am nothing, and without me, the people have no link, no emissary to her. As I gaze upon the temple's intricately carved facade, a surge of pride wells within me. The locket's power brought me here, letting me see through the eyes of someone important to her community, someone with a value beyond herself.

I enter the temple, the air heavy with the scent of burning incense. Pillars of stone surround me, adorned with symbols of divinity. As I move further within, the dim light reveals an altar of offerings where prayers are whispered and destinies entwined.

In the heart of the temple, I stand before an ancient mirror. Its reflective, light blue-hued surface shimmered with an ethereal light. At first, I see myself as Ishtar's priestess. But the more I look into it, the more my reflection shifts. I come to see myself in the present day, in my pajamas, sitting in the Memory Room.

With a graceful movement, I lightly tap one finger on the mirror's surface. It responds with a ripple of energy, and before my eyes, scenes from my life as Ishtar's priestess dance like phantoms in the mist. I witness rituals honoring the gods, dances telling stories of creation, and moments of connection between mortals and the divine.

As the mirror's visions fade, I feel a sense of awe and wonder unlike anything I had ever experienced. I stand on the precipice of a civilization's golden age, feeling the pulse of humanity's dreams and aspirations. In Mesopotamia's embrace, I've discovered a connection transcending time itself.

With a final glance, I step away from the mirror, and the scene warps back to the ziggurat's summit. I sit on the top step. The sun has set, no longer casting a warm glow upon the city. The locket rests in my hand, but I can't be sure if it is in the memory or if reality and the vision have melded. The city is black aside from the fires glowing, dotting the architecture in various sconces and braziers. The sounds from early have all but gone away. I can hear singing from behind me in the ziggurat's grand temple. I stand up and turn around, intending to join the festivities, but a shadow rushes over me.

I'm forced back into the farmhouse. My heart is racing, but still, I feel the locket's power offering glimpses into the tapestry of human existence spanning millennia. With a newfound reverence, I hold the locket close against my chest, knowing now that each vision may unlock knowledge and deepen my understanding of our history.

The memories of Mesopotamia are still vivid in my mind, still fresh. Am I a freak now, walking around with memories of a time ten thousand years before my own existence? The locket feels warm against my palm, my link to a time long past. I remain in this safe corner of the room, the weight of what I experienced settling upon me.

I closed my eyes, letting it all wash over me once again. I can almost hear the bustling streets, the chants of the priests, and the whispers of ancient wisdom. It's as if I had momentarily stepped into a different reality, witnessing a chapter of human history that had shaped the course of civilization.

As I opened my eyes, the locket glinted in the light. It

was already closed, its twisting floral design mirroring the mysteries it held within. I know now countless stories and lifetimes are waiting to be explored through its power. Each memory contains something new, something exciting to discover. Amelia's memory taught me to reach out to others when I need help. I think this one is telling me to be of value to the community, to add something to the lives of others, instead of hiding myself away in this house.

With reverence and anticipation, I hold the locket to my chest. The journey I have embarked upon is strange, and I don't yet understand it. As I gaze out the window at the tranquil, moonlit landscape of the farmhouse, I know more stories are waiting to be told. With the locket as my guide, I believe I'm ready to delve deeper into this mystery, this strange room, this mighty artifact, and the odyssey of humankind spanning millennia.

Ethan McGrane

Chapter 8

Knocking Door, Ringing Phone

The morning unfolds with a grumble from my stomach, an immediate reminder of yesterday's forgotten task — grocery shopping. Regret whispers its familiar tune, chastising me for my oversight. As I dress, a mental checklist of items I need forms. I vow not to repeat the same mistake. To succeed in my current endeavor, I must balance the demands of mundanity with pursuing the extraordinary journey I've embarked upon.

I examine myself in the bathroom mirror. Should I add the blazer to my black slacks and buttoned blue shirt, or do I only want to look sort of like I'm ready for a day at the office? I'll have to remember to get laundry detergent at the store today. I'm out of my non-business-casual attire.

When I'm putting on the finishing touches for my expedition today, somebody knocks at the door. I'm not expecting guests today. The unknown party knocks again as I descend the stairs. Opening the front door reveals Cedric from the diner yesterday morning. He's still eccentrically dressed. It must be a coincidence, but the shirt he is wearing with his russet-colored linen suit is the same material and color blue as the shirt I'm wearing now.

"Good morning, Emma."

I reciprocate his greeting, but it seems too early in the morning for me to act convincingly typical. Cedric, though, decides to get to the point.

"I wanted to swing by this morning to–"

My phone rings, cutting him off. I look down, it's Gerald. I ask Cedric to excuse me and then retreat to the study. I sink into the desk chair I bought and press the green button on my phone screen.

"Hello," I answer.

"Ten days, Emmy. Haven't heard from you in ten days. I was fixin' to report you missin'."

"I know, I know. Sorry. I'm having a hard time. Mandy died."

"Christ, I'm sorry." He says. "Where are you? You kept duckin' my calls, so I called your building. They said you haven't been there in over a week, and your office said the same thing."

"I'm in Maine. I bought an old farmhouse. I'm working remotely and fixing the house in my free time."

"You don't know the first thing about fixin' a house!"

Surprised at his outrage, I pause momentarily, "You're right."

"Lemme come up and help you. Text me the address."

"Alright. But I have to go now. I was in the middle of something when you called."

"Don't forget to send me the address."

I swipe my finger across the screen to end the call. My mind is in limbo between welcoming Gerald into this mysterious realm and the harsh reality of unraveling my secret—the Memory Room. Will his practical mind discern the intricacies of this esoteric chamber, or will his disdain for the paranormal shatter the delicate illusion I've so carefully crafted? Gerald, the skeptic, once scoffed at my ghostly sighting in our childhood home's living room, retorting with a brusque "piss off."

I cut through the clutter of furniture I've yet to organize in the living room. The front door comes into my line of sight, but I don't see Cedric. These men shoe-horning themselves into my new life are going to drive me insane.

Entering the foyer, I don't have to call out for Cedric. The russet-colored shape of a man is halfway up the stairs, looking around in a manner a typical person would only employ for comedic effect. I clear my throat to get his attention.

"Sorry, I thought I heard something up there."

Immediately, my mind conjures the memories of my first day in this house, how the whisper called to me. Is the Memory Room beckoning Cedric now? I can't have anyone else in this house until I get to the bottom of the locket and its power.

"It's an old house. There's a lot of weird noises. Say, I was about to go to Danny's. Maybe we can talk about whatever you want to talk about over breakfast?"

"Certainly," Cedric says. "I can drive us there if you'd like?"

"I have some errands to run afterward. I'll meet you at the diner," I say, opening the door.

Cedric smiles and leaves.

***

"Do you mind if I smoke?" Cedric asks.

"Not at all," I lie. "But, I looked it up. Maine doesn't allow smoking in indoor public places."

"I have a knack for getting away with things like this." Cedric smiles and produces from the pocket on the interior of his suit jacket a turquoise pack of cigarettes with a cartoon Native American silhouetted on the front and a zippo lighter. The lighter is a dark nickel color, and engraved on the

47

front is what looks like a pentagram, but with extra lines and circles. Cedric is from somewhere beyond my understanding. When I drove away from Boston, I wasn't expecting to arrive in a more complicated world. City life is often busy, but South Boston has nothing on South Thornbrook.

Before Cedric can take the first drag of his cigarette, Tiff greets us as jovially as usual. "Well, hey there, you two! Glad to see the two newcomers to town settling in here."

The revelation that Cedric is also new in town caught me off guard. Before, his effortless interactions and confident demeanor disarmed me. I feel like a fish out of water, so I follow the people who look like they know what they're doing to survive. Every revelation adds another layer of mystery to the small town's intricacies. I wonder what brings him to this seemingly forgotten place. The shared status of "newcomer" sparks a silent camaraderie, a connection forged amid the enigma of South Thornbrook.

I order my favorite breakfast – black coffee, one over-easy egg, two pieces of crispy turkey bacon, and home fries.

"Same meal two mornings in a row?" Cedric asks.

"I'm a creature of habit," I say, testing the temperature of my coffee with an experimental sip.

"Not one for sugar or cream?" Cedric asks.

"I keep things simple, to the point."

Cedric orders a glass of orange juice and two pieces of whole wheat toast. Tiff smiles, pivots to the left on her tennis shoe, and retreats to her solitude behind the bar, passing the ticket from her notepad to the kitchen window.

"Sorry for rushing you out of the house earlier. I hadn't had anything to eat since I left here yesterday morning." I say.

"Quite alright, Miss Green. You should take better care of yourself." His accent and mannerisms are so foreign. I'm not sure how he knows my full name, either.

"Just 'Emma' will do. So, what did you want to talk

to me about when you dropped by this morning?" I ask.

"Well, *Emma*, I'm a New England Historical Society member. The house you now own, I believe, has a history– A long and storied but ultimately untold history. By purchasing tools and furniture, I believe you intend to restore the house. I want to document the house's restoration, with your permission, of course."

"I don't think there's anything noteworthy at the house. It's an old farmhouse. The barn isn't even standing anymore. And the last owners didn't leave anything behind that I've found."

I can't have him poking around the house. Why can't I? Even if he does find the Memory Room, all I have to do is have the locket hidden away. The locket is the vital part, not the room. I could say I don't know why someone built a room in the attic or the purpose of the chair and table. The room could be a reading room or a hideaway for one of the previous owners. I don't know why I have such an urge to hide the Memory Room.

"You know, why not? Sure, you can record the restoration."

"Thank you, Ms. Gre– I'm sorry, Emma. Even if you haven't missed anything in the house, the house itself is a relic, and it deserves chronicling, both the current state after years of neglect and its future after this transition phase. Regardless, this will be of no cost to you, and maybe you can look back on it later with a fondness for the work you put into the house to save it.

50

Chapter 9

NECS

The following morning, Cedric arrives while my new coffee maker finishes its first brew. His suit is slightly lighter than my coffee, and his shirt is yellow as mustard. Where did he get his sense of style?

I usher Cedric inside and invite him to the kitchen, where I pour my coffee and ask him if he would like some. "No, thank you," He says.

From the inside pocket of his jacket, he produces a tri-folded paper. "This is a general contract. I'm required by the NECS to have you sign it before I can render any official services," He says.

"What does it entail?" I ask. I'm a little put off by the contract. I wasn't expecting something so formal and binding. Is this a scam? No, it can't be a scam.

"It's a simple contract," Cedric says, not reassuring me much. "The New England Chroniclers Society is a non-profit entity. We do not owe you any compensation for chronicling your home or any items found within your property, nor do you owe us any compensation for our services."

I skim over the contract. It looks official enough, and the contents match the details he said, so I sign it. We begin with the first floor once the formality is out of the way. Cedric asks about the house's original features. I don't know anything about the house's history. The only thing I have to work with are assumptions. The house has been on the market for seven years, but I think it's been vacant much longer. I have a feeling Cedric will ask many questions I don't have the answers for.

"What's in the basement?" Cedric asks.

"Washer, dryer, well, water heater, and some empty shelves," I answer.

"I think we can skip the basement, then." He says.

Ascending the stairs, I remember my hideaway in the attic. If Cedric goes up there, he'll see the locket. Will he take it with him for 'chronicling,' or worse, will the Guardian step in and stop him?

We go through the two bedrooms, but there's nothing noteworthy.

I stop in front of the door to my bedroom. "Please excuse the mess," I say.

"I promise not to judge. I know how it is to live out of a suitcase," He says.

I open the door to let Cedric go about his business. He takes pictures of the walls, runs his finger along the window sill, and shifts his weight on an exceptionally creaky floorboard. The verdict? Nothing remarkable in here, either.

Cedric can't hide his disappointment, his facial features have gradually turned downwards throughout our trek. On our way back to the steps, he sees the scuff marks on the floor underneath the pull-down stairs to the attic.

He glances to the ceiling trapdoor and then to me, "Is there anything up there?"

"It's an attic," I answer. I aim for a nonchalant tone, but my terror at him discovering the Memory Room botches my intention. "There's a little reading room up there," I try to recover from the previous sentence's waver.

My heart pounds in sync with our steps up the rickety stairs, but what I see when we get to the attic almost makes me faint.

The Memory Room is gone. I have to question my sanity. I wonder if I hallucinated the room in this attic, the Guardian, the locket, the visions... everything. I begin to wonder if the last week of my life was simply some grief-fueled psychotic trip. All of my thoughts halt when I notice Cedric's surprise. Is it a surprise, or am I reading him wrong? He could just be confused that I said there was a nonexistent room up here.

Cedric regains his bearing. We descend to the second floor, and he helps me fold the stairs back into the ceiling. Though I'll be coming back here in a few moments, it's easier for me to pull the stairs back down again than to think of an excuse for returning to an empty attic.

Cedric says farewell, tapping his phone and saying his work is cut out for tonight. As he's walking away, I can't help but wonder if he's got work to do chronicling the house or if he's going to contemplate the disappearance of the Memory Room. I also want answers to that, but I have a direct line to those answers. Cedric does not.

Chapter 10

"You Are Crazy"

From the porch, I watch Cedric's sedan disappear over my driveway's first hill. I turn around and reenter the house. It feels weird having had another person in this house. Aside from the Guardian, I've been the only one here since I bought the mysterious Oak Cove House.

I stop in the kitchen to take a sip of my coffee. It's already cold. Heading for the attic, I loop around the hallway, take the stairs to the second floor, and pull down the steps for the attic. The Memory Room is back to where it should be. As if in a horror movie, the hinges creak as the door slowly swings open for me. My heart races at the sight. I swear under my breath and enter the room.

"Why did you do that?" I ask.

I don't like that man. I don't trust him.

"Neither do I, yet," I say, trying to empathize with the Guardian.

Then you shouldn't have let him in the house.

"You made me look like a crazy person."

You are crazy. Otherwise, you would have run away from this house when you started hearing voices and reliving memories from your past lives.

Before I say anything else, I realize the Guardian is right. Any ordinary person would have left at the first whiff of anything paranormal. Well, an average person wouldn't have bought this house. Maybe I have made a mistake.

You didn't make a mistake. The locket, the wealth of knowledge, the emotions, the experiences within it, all of it can help you. Nobody who understands that potential would shun the opportunity. The more you discover, the more I may know why I'm trapped here.

"You're right. But don't hide the room anymore. I'm perfectly capable of handling this. I told Cedric there was a reading room up here, and I could have said the locket was one of my family heirlooms."

I will leave the room here, but be careful who you bring here. That locket is the only thing that can give me answers, and you're the only one I trust to use it.

I sit in the chair and flip the locket in my hand over a few times. I don't have anything else to do today. I might as well use the locket more, and get closer to unraveling this enigma I've stumbled upon in my desperation to outrun grief.

I click open the locket and look into the eyes of the portrait trapped within the silver shell. I wait for the sensation to overtake me. I wait to be drawn into the portal to another life. After a few moments, nothing happens.

It won't work in the daytime. Sunlight nullifies its power.

"I'll come back tonight, then."

As I exit the room, repulsion wells beneath my palette, ready to erupt in a disgusted retch. If I am crazy, I'm not going to let the voice in the attic tell me otherwise.

***

The night air slices through the open window, a chilling accomplice to my escape. Three miles out of South Thornbrook, I press the gas pedal harder, the engine's growl matching my escalating panic. I don't intend to return to the house, especially not to the Memory Room. The road stretches like an uncertain path through thick woods, shadows conspiring with the night. The wheels beneath me seem to turn with the grind of fate, destination unknown.

But as the hollow miles unfold, a dissonant symphony pierces the eerie calm—a ringing, an unbearable wail echoing not just in my ears but through the very core of my being. It's as if the spectral forces of the Oak Cove House have forged an ethereal tether to my fleeing soul. The ringing claws into my sanity, demanding recognition.

In the car's confines, panic and the rhythmic thud of my heart against my ribs collide. The night engulfs me, the road stretching endlessly, and the ringing, a relentless siren's call, refuses to fade. Panic transforms into determination. I can't escape the spectral grasp if the tendrils of the unknown still cling to me.

With a whirl of gravel and desperation, I bang a U-turn from one shoulder to the other, the car heading back towards South Thornbrook. The darkness melds with the unnatural hum, shrouding the road in an otherworldly glow. The miles unravel beneath my tires, dread coiling around my heart. The Guardian, a silent specter from the Memory Room, now feels like a relentless pursuer across the dim stretches of road.

A macabre waltz unfolds—a lone car cutting through the thick night, a sole driver entwined with forces beyond comprehension. I race back towards the unknown, the Guardian of the Memory Room asserting dominion over more than just the confines of Oak Cove House. The ringing persists, a phantom melody dictating the tempo of my escape or, perhaps, my surrender to the enigma that now binds my fate.

I need to give the Guardian what he wants. Otherwise, I'll never leave South Thornbrook again.

Chapter 11

Alessandra De Medici

During the forty-five-minute drive home, my defeat over being unable to escape this house morphed into resolve to overcome the challenge. I must work within the parameters given to me: use the locket, find out why the locket is here, and help the Guardian.

The locket's weight rests against my palm. I close my eyes, inhale deeply, open the locket, exhale slowly, and then open my eyes. The transition is much smoother. If my first time using the locket was like trying to stream a video on dial-up internet, now it's like using high-speed wifi to watch an entire movie.

I let the modern world fade, and when the darkness is replaced by a new vision, I'm standing amidst the grandeur of Renaissance Florence, Italy. The city's bustling streets are alive with merchants hawking their wares, and the melodies of street performers flood my ears.

My attire has transformed into sumptuous garments, opulently flowing like water. A sense of excitement pulses through me as I move through the cobblestone streets. I am but a passenger along for this ride. I have become unable to resist these adventures, these guided tours of times long gone. I am drawn to a grand building, a symbol of power and prestige—an elegant bank run by the Medici family.

As I step inside, I'm met with a symphony of sounds—the rustling of parchment, the clinking of coins, and the murmurs of hushed conversations. I'm a woman of influence, a banker with a sharp mind and keen business sense. A portrait on the wall catches my eye—it's me, or rather, the woman whose mind I occupy, a forgotten Medici banker who shares a connection with my present-day life as an accountant.

Through the bank's hallowed halls, I glide with practiced ease, a regal figure commanding the attention of clients and orchestrating the intricate dance of financial transactions. Her memories, a torrential river, cascade into my consciousness—endless hours immersed in the tomes of ledgers, the sharp negotiations that wove fortunes like an alchemist brewing elixirs of prosperity.

Yet it's not the record of professional triumphs that strikes the chords within, but the glimpses into the hidden chambers of her soul. The echoes of laughter dancing in the company of friends, the solitary moments bathed in the soft glow of flickering candles, and the yearning for a life steeped in the rich brew of love and purpose. The symphony of her existence plays not in the grandiose halls of achievement but in the intimate recesses where joy, solitude, and the relentless pursuit of a meaningful existence converge.

I can feel her, really *feel* Alessandra right now. Her thoughts are racing through my mind as she looks back on her life. A memory stands out—a moonlit evening, a secret rendezvous with a kindred spirit who sees beyond the facade of power and recognizes the vulnerability beneath. As I experience this memory, tears blur my vision. Alessandra buries herself in her work to distract herself from losing her true love.

Back in the farmhouse, I hold the locket close, its surface warm against my skin. Alessandra De Medici's spirit lingers within me, a reminder that the enigma of the past mirrors the echoes of our own lives. In her story, I see a reflection of my journey as an accountant, navigating a world that demands precision and expertise.

It never works out. You can't distract yourself from sadness, not that kind of sadness. No obsession will ever suffice. Six hundred years later, and your soul still hasn't learned that.

"What's your point?" I ask.

Obsession wears many masks.

"I'm not obsessed with anything. I'm trying to help you, and fix this house."

Alessandra thought she could drown her sorrows in her work... Distractions only mask the grief... They don't eliminate it.

I cross my arms in front of me. "I'm not trying to distract myself. I just need something to focus on.

Mandy's loss echoes in these walls. You hide from the pain, but it lingers. What would occupy you if you weren't distracting yourself?

My jaw tightens as I remember what I did for those days following the building collapse. "I can't just sit around and mourn forever."

Alessandra thought so, too. Yet her every accomplishment felt hollow because of a love lost.

My skin burns, tears welling in my eyes. "What are you getting at?

You bury yourself, but it won't resurrect what's gone.

The tears escape my eyes with my outburst, "Stop comparing me to her!

Alessandra realized too late the ghosts she sought to banish became the walls of her self-made prison.

Trembling, I say, not sure of who I'm trying to

convince anymore, "I'm not... I'm not hiding.

Acknowledge the ghosts, or you'll become one yourself.

I leap from the chair and bolt toward the exit. I expected the door to slam shut or disappear. The Guardian let me go with one last tidbit as a parting gift.

The path to liberation begins with acceptance.

Chapter 12

Drained

Rolling over, I glare at the cursed timepiece. The digits sneer back, declaring an hour that mocks the disciplined rhythm of my past. 1:07 PM, a betrayal of the sun's zenith, and I, who once rose with the dawn, now lay entangled in the shackles of a merciless slumber. A lethargy not born of rest but conceived in the shadowed corners of an unrestful mind.

A lifetime of early awakenings shattered in one morning. For years, daybreak was my confidant. Now, I've lost my well-practiced routine. I grapple with disbelief. How did I relinquish the reins to this tempest of sleep? The indignant clock ticks as if it knows the gravity of its defiance. Once a sanctuary of respite, the bed now cradles me in an unfamiliar afternoon embrace.

In a whirlwind of disoriented panic, I catapult myself from the bed, the sheets tangling in my hastened ascent. The ghostly light of a day lived without my witness casts a pallor over the room, mocking the discipline I had prided myself on for years. My fumbling hand snatches my cell phone.

Gerald's attempts to reach me are scrawled across the screen. Three missed calls from my older brother and a solitary message begging for a lifeline. His words, terse yet laden with love, beckon me to surrender the isolation I have wrapped myself in. "Don't shut me out," the words linger, not merely a plea but a command. He ends the message with a promise, "Just send me your address, and I'll be there for you."

With a swipe, I banish the notification into the digital void. I know it's only a feeble attempt to postpone the reckoning with Gerald's imminent arrival. He won't let up until he has his way. The specter of his presence looms on the horizon, a guest threatening the fragile facade that shields me from the world. In the seclusion of my domain, where shadows dance with the ghosts of my past, I find solace in the distractions of the Memory Room. Yet, I grapple with the unsettling reality that the refuge I have built might crumble in the face of Gerald's well-intentioned intrusion.

I get out of bed and take inventory. Headache? Check. Nausea? Check. Joint Stiffness? Check. I stretch, yawn, and get dressed for the day. Gray shirt, black jeans, I'm ready for my afternoon of killing time. Maybe I'll check my email, listen to a podcast, read a book… I don't know. I just need to pass the time until dusk to use the locket again.

Eager anticipation courses through the sinews of my spine. The unexplored beckons, promising new odysseys. I've witnessed the allure of the Renaissance in Florence, Italy, with its cobblestone streets whispering artistry. I've traversed the gritty landscapes of 1960s New York City, where the pulse of a generation reverberated through the streets. And, in the shadowy corridors of history, I've tread upon the ancient soil of the primarily forgotten Sumerian City of Eridu, a testament to the layers of time that shroud the secrets of civilizations past.

Anyone can visualize, but my eyes have seen outside of my lifetime. Like worms writhing in mud, my thoughts hold my attention. Their movements and motives are alien to me. My head holds memories from people who perished millennia ago. Perhaps I overslept today because my body needs the energy to transform, to ascend. Maybe I'm reaching a higher consciousness. I'm becoming more human than the typical human. With the locket, I can acquire knowledge and wisdom outside of my lifetime. Maybe that's what the Guardian was trying to tell me last night. I can learn from the mistakes my antecessors made.

Ethan McGrane

Chapter 13

Mourning in Skiringssal

8:37, the sun has sufficiently descended past the horizon, and my conduit to another life can now be activated. I can't resist this urge, the buzzing at the back of my skull, my shallow breaths. What will I see next? I open the locket and close my eyes. The world around me dissolves, and I find myself standing amid a village of wooden houses. The air is crisp, scents of wood and earth swirling around me.

My attire is simple. My ankle-length dress of rough beige fabric rests on the top of my worn, untreated leather shoes. A pale blue apron covers from my collar bones to right below my knees. My wardrobe is a reflection of my simple life as a farmer. My braided hair hangs over my left shoulder, and I smooth back the stray hairs on top of my head with my labor-calloused hands. I follow her gaze to a humble house on the outskirts of town, a large field sitting behind it. In the front yard, a group of mourners gather. The emotions coursing through this mind are intense and unrelenting. I can feel all of her thoughts in pristine detail.

My husband has passed away, his life claimed by an infected wound he sustained while gathering firewood. I feel

Astrid's grief as though it were my own. The weight of responsibility settling on her shoulders threatens to crush her. As she stands amidst the mourners, I feel a connection to her sorrow, a recognition of loss that echoes across time.

Astrid moves with purpose, preparing for the funeral. Her hands tremble as she fastens the brooch onto her husband's collar, her thoughts a whirlwind of emotions. Amidst her grief, I catch glimpses of determination—a fierce resolve to carry on, to provide for her six children and tend to the farm they once worked together.

The village's support surrounds Astrid, a community rallying to help her in her time of need. As stones are set upon her husband's grave to create a small burial mound, Astrid muses how the rocks are a perfect metaphor for the heaviness of her heart. But Astrid's eyes remain dry, her strength unwavering. She's not just mourning. I sense her mind churning, considering how she will take on the responsibilities that were once shared.

In the days following the funeral, I follow along with Astrid's every step. She tends to the farm, feeding livestock and tending to crops. Her days are long and demanding, but there's a rhythm to her actions, a determination that propels her forward. She rises with the sun, her children by her side, teaching them the skills they'll need to survive.

As the seasons shift, so does Astrid's resolve. I feel her grief ebbing away, replaced by a deep sense of purpose. She's not just managing; she's thriving. I witness her ingenious strategies— negotiating trades, bartering goods, and forming alliances with fellow villagers. Her determination is unyielding, and her strength is infectious.

Years later, Astrid sits along its shore as the sun sets over the fjord. Her reflection dances in the water. Her hair has grayed, and when she splashes her hands along the surface, her fingers are knurled with arthritis. I sense more than a physical transformation. Her grief blossomed into a sense of self-assurance, an unwavering commitment to her remaining family.

Astrid's thoughts turn to her children, their laughter echoing throughout her memories. She's taught them the values of hard work and resilience, passing down the knowledge that sustained her family and culture for countless generations. Her husband's presence is felt in every step she has taken since his funeral. Arve continues to live on in the dirt beneath Astrid's fingernails.

We gaze toward the horizon, a mixture of grief and determination infecting our minds. Astrid is a testament to the power of the human spirit to overcome even the darkest of challenges. Still, despite all the fury, all the resolve to carry on and live without he who she thought she would have forever, Astrid is only human. Tears well in her eyes as she watches the sun touch the waters at the edge of the world. A shadow dances over the fjord, whisking me back to the farmhouse.

With the locket's power still pulsing within me, my fingers wrapped around its cold surface. Tears streaming down my face. The memory of Astrid lingers. I take a deep breath, drawing strength from her example, knowing that as I face my challenges and grief, I'll carry Astrid's spirit. She'll be a beacon of resolve. Her journey applies to mine. As Astrid found the strength to carry on and thrive, I must learn to navigate a world no longer occupied by those I considered most important. Astrid's resilience can be a blueprint for finding purpose and strength amidst loss.

Did the locket grant me Astrid's story on purpose? Does it know I grieve? The Memory Room lent me an insight into the resilience of the human spirit. Astrid's story reminds me that even in sorrow, there's a way to find strength and forge ahead. I dry my eyes with my sleeve.

You've seen the echoes of loss and grief, the ache of parting that reverberates through the corridors of time.

"It's a never-ending cycle of pain."

But in that cycle, do you not see the strength of those who endure? The resilience of the human spirit?

"I guess so. People seem to manage to go on, even when it feels impossible."

Life is fleeting, Emma. People, connections, moments—they are the threads that weave the tapestry of existence. Cherish them.

"I get it. I've been too caught up in the past, in what I've lost."

The past can be a heavy burden, but it shouldn't blind you to the richness of the present. Gerald, your brother, the memories you're creating now—they are the treasures of today.

"You're right. I need to value what's here and now."

Life is a mosaic of fleeting moments. Treasure each shard, for together they form a masterpiece. Don't sacrifice what you have, for what you once had.

I leave the room. My mind whirls as I descend the stairs. I'm supposed to be the one helping the Guardian, but now it seems our relationship has reversed. I can't push the people who love me away. I text Gerald my address. The people in our lives are valuable. Nobody can be replaced, only cherished while they are here, and mourned when they are gone.

Chapter 14

The Prognosis

I sit the stack of thriller novels on the table in the Memory Room. I picked them out of a bargain bin at the supermarket. I haven't read much but a few pages, but their purpose today isn't for reading. It's for obscuring. I pocket the locket and move toward the exit of the room. I can already hear my brother's exaggerated Boston accent.

Put it back, the Guardian demands. I'm afraid I have no choice but to oblige, so I open one of the novels and sit it upside down over the locket. Gerald will be here for a while. I've already talked it over with the Guardian. He was reluctant to allow a long-term guest, but I told him without Gerald fixing the house, the whole thing would likely fall over within the next few years. Ultimately, the Guardian chose temporary discomfort over the risk of losing his home.

I've got the spirit's promise: no slamming doors, no disappearing rooms, no weird sounds or eerie presences. As if on cue, as soon as I had the Guardian's word that he'd leave my brother alone, I heard a V8 engine approaching the house.

I open the front door to the house as Gerald pulls his

suitcase from the backseat of his truck. His truck is his freedom. He could never work for anybody for an extended time. He always has to do things his way. As a general contractor, he can do almost any job. The problem with him being a day's drive away from his hometown is that he doesn't have friends around who can do the jobs he can't.

After he hoists his suitcase up the two steps to the porch, he says, "Come here, Emmy," and ambushes me with a bear hug.

"Sorry about Mandy. She was good people," He says.

"Not now," I reply.

After a few more seconds of embrace, he finally lets go. I guide him into the living room. He will likely be sleeping on the couch here for a bit, as no furniture is suitable for sleeping in the rest of the house. I would offer him my bed, as I spend most nights in the Memory Room lately, but I think Gerald will become suspicious if I disappear to the attic every night.

"Let's take a look around the place real quick. We should get on the same page about what needs doing here," Gerald says.

"You'll know best. This is how you make your living. I just want the house updated while preserving the heritage," I say.

"Since when did you care about heritage?" Gerald says.

I shrug.

Gerald slides the bottom of his boot along the floor. "The floohs are gonna have to be sanded and refinished, but that'll come later, one of the last things on the list, so we don't have to worry bout the flooh while we're doing the rest of the wawk."

We go into the living room. "You married to the fireplace? It could cause some issues latah on."

I hadn't thought anything was wrong with the

chimney. "I want it to stay."

"Easiah that way."

He runs his hand along the wall, taps on it a few times, and grabs the hammer I had left on the window sill in the study. I can't remember why I put it there or what I used it for, but everything has been blurring outside of the Memory Room.

"We're gonna have to redo the walls anyway, so 'scuse this," Gerald says.

"Excuse what?" I ask. I was too late to ask, as Gerald does what he's best at, and put a hole in the wall. The noise made me jump, but I wasn't angry or disappointed at the damage. He's here to fix the house, after all.

"Yeah, we're gonna have to redo all the drywall. It's all brittle and lookin' kinda funky under that wallpaper. Plus, nobody uses laths anymore, so we'll take those down. The studs are gettin' up there in age, so we'll reinforce the load bearin' walls at the very least." Gerald turns the hammer around, stabs it claw-first into the drywall, and leaves it hanging as though it was a normal thing to do.

Gerald opens and closes the exterior door at the back of the hallway a few times. "You're gonna need all new doors and windows. These are old as shit."

"Tell me how you really feel," I joke.

"You want your new place fixed up, or you want me to be a therapist?" He replies.

We go to the kitchen. Gerald glances around and sees the stack of paper plates, foam bowls, and the two coffee mugs I got at the corner store. "Why's the kitchen so nice?"

"I thought the same thing when I saw it for the first time, too," I say.

"Rest of the house looks twenty years out of date. But this kitchen looks like I helped build it in high school."

"So, still really old?"

Gerald squints at me. Then goes back to talking. "It's

fine, but with your taste, you'll probably want new cabinets and countertops. We'll take that gawdawful bulkhead out from over the cabinets, and you can decide whether you want full-height cabinets or empty space. Every kitchen I've remodeled in the last ten years has had me take the damn soffits out."

"I wasn't a fan of them. They make the room feel smaller," I say.

"Exactly."

The dining room was next on the tour. Gerald mused about the table, how he can picture "all of us," which I assume means his family plus me, "sittin' round the table for Thanksgiving or something." I'm glad my big brother is making plans for my house already.

"There a bathroom down heeuh?" Gerald asks.

"There is, but it doesn't work."

"Where at?"

"Under the stairs."

"I'll take a look latah. Let's head upstairs." Gerald says.

I was starting to get bored, so I stopped paying attention. The walls, the floors, the windows, all of those had to be replaced. The bedrooms were nice, but they had two different closet styles: one was bifold, and the other was a standard hinged door. I hadn't thought anything was weird about that.

The master bedroom got the same verdict as everything else, "gut it, and build it back better."

Gerald points to the attic entrance in the upstairs hall and says, "You probably don't care how that looks."

"Actually, I've been using a nice little room up there as a reading space."

Gerald turns up his bottom lip slightly and nods. "Cool, I'll check it later, see what needs doin'. Let's check the cellah."

"Actually, I've got to get to something real quick, work-related," that's a lie. I'm just tired of waltzing around the house with him. I return to my room and grab one of my checkbooks. Handing the checks to Gerald, I tell him, "There's around two hundred and fifty thousand dollars in this account. Will that be enough?"

"I could teah the whole house down and rebuild it, maybe twice with that kinda doh." He says.

"Good. You know what I want, and you know what you're doing. What's the prognosis?"

"Two weeks to a month, but no more than six weeks. I'm not missin' Liam's birthday. Five's a big one." He says.

"Get this house in order, and I'll come down for his birthday, too."

"You got it," Gerald says, then goes downstairs. Of course, he hadn't resolved everything in his head until he was in the foyer.

"Ay!" He shouts up to me.

"Yes?" I call back to him.

"Gas station down the street's runnin' a deal on chicken tonight. Least that's what the sign said. I'm gonna pick some up for suppah."

"Just let me know when you're going, and I'll give you some cash for it," I say.

"What am I? Twelve? I wasn't askin' for cash. Just wanted to make sure you were good with it." He says.

"I'm not picky," I say.

"Yes, you are."

Chapter 15

In Memoriam

My alarm goes off at nine the following morning. I snooze it and rollover. I don't feel like getting up. I don't feel rested. I'm sore. I kept tossing and turning, waking up just to go back to sleep. But if I wait until one in the afternoon to get out of bed, I will beat myself up over it. Gerald would probably worry about me more than he already is if I slept all day.

All night, I had nightmares about the locket. The police showed up, kicked down my door, and hauled me off to a clean white room. Staff in pristine white uniforms would mill about coming in and out of my cell. Occasionally, they would drag me into a different room, sit me at a table, and berate me. They would tell me things like "The Guardian isn't real," "The Memory Room doesn't exist," "The locket is just a piece of jewelry," and "There's no such thing as magic." Their insistence would turn into frustration and anger. Eventually, it devolved into me shouting, "I'm not crazy!" and a choir of healthcare workers shouting, "Yes, you are!" back at me.

The dream ended with me sitting alone in my room.

Through the door, I could see Gerald and Cedric. Gerald shook his head and walked away. Cedric put his hand on the annealed glass window. He glances over his shoulder a few times, double-checking each direction down the hallway, and then he reaches into the breast pocket of his blazer and holds up the locket.

I've never been in a mental institution. Do they even exist anymore? My only frame of reference is that movie from the late 1980s. What was the name of it? The doctor in charge of the facility had a portal to hell. Oh well, it's not essential. I'm letting my mind wander too much and paying too much credit to a dream. I need to get up and start my day.

Commencing my customary morning walkthrough of the house, I discover I'm home alone. Gerald must have got up early. I wonder what he'll start working on first? I don't know where I would start, so I'm glad he's here.

While my coffee was brewing, I stepped over to the still out-of-order restroom and used the mirror to put my hair in a loose bun. The bags under my eyes are getting worse.

The coffee maker hisses its death knell, and I retrieve my ambrosia, bringing it to the desk in the study across the hall from the kitchen. I've liked this desk a lot more since Henry told me about the lawyer who had this as a vacation home. This desk has a very commanding aura. It's a desk a president should be sitting behind, not one that should have rotted away in an abandoned farmhouse. I might have Gerald refinish it and get a glass top to protect it.

I flip the lid of my laptop open and enter my password. While waiting for it to boot, I take a small test sip of my coffee, which is still too hot for human consumption. Once the laptop has booted, I open the web browser and navigate to my email. The first one is a memo from the CEO of my company, announcing the tragic passing of Amanda Wright and a mail room intern.

Whatever momentum I was building for this morning,

getting ready to power through my work, read the reports, flag any errors my subordinates may have made, or anything that looks bad for the company revenue reports… all the things that take focus. I've lost the will to do it.

The day unfurls before me, vast and unclaimed, yet my motivation lies dormant. My laptop, bearer of tasks, leers at me with its demands, but it's merely a Tuesday. There is abundant time to satisfy my employer's needs. Folding the device shut, I surrender to the comforting embrace of my chair, its plush depths a refuge. In this quiet, thoughts, once suppressed by clamor, rise like specters from the recesses of my mind. Can I endure the storm of self-reflection? I long for a distraction to save me from the mental battlefield.

As if to answer my prayers, the sound of a diesel engine hums through the house. I rise from my chair and go to the living room window. It's a rather large truck, now making a three-point turn in my driveway. I exit the house to investigate further.

I stand on the porch, and the driver waves at me as soon as I catch his eye. He shouts something at me, but I can't hear him over the engine. I just nod at him. I listen to him shift the truck into park, and air releases from the brakes. The driver hops down and goes to a series of levers on the side, right behind the cab.

The green-painted, half-rusted steel box on the back of the truck lifts up in front first and then begins to slide off the rear. Gerald wasted no time in getting a roll-off dumpster. I'm sure he's out on the town right now, organizing things for the upcoming restoration.

Leaning against one of the posts on the porch, I cross my arms and watch the driver detach the dumpster, chock the side facing downhill, and then return his truckbed to its normal position. He just waves at me, "Have a good one," then gets back in the truck and leaves.

I return to the study, still waiting to feel like doing

something. My coffee has gone cold, and so has my motivation. I'll just sit here until something compels me to do otherwise. I will look into retirement options as soon as I get this house fixed. I've had enough of this life so far. My previous ones were more interesting and consequential.

Two days without the locket, and I'm missing it. The wonder, excitement, and intrigue make me wish I was sitting in the attic now. I disengage my elbows from the desk and rub my temples as I sink back into the chair.

With timing so perfect I would assume he planned it, Gerald walks through the front door as soon as I feel relaxed.

"I'm home," he shouts.

"Welcome back," I call back to him, trying not to sound annoyed.

"I see the dumpstah got here,"

I'm unsure if he wants an answer, so I don't respond.

"What's the mattah with you?" Gerald asks, poking his head in from the living room.

"They sent out Mandy's *In Memoriam* today," I say.

Gerald disappears back to the living room. Thanks for the support. Maybe I don't need Gerald's help in my emotional matters. Surely, I can work through this on my own. Why did an email hit me so hard? What did that email do that undid the work I put into distancing myself from the tragedy?

The Guardian, if he could speak to me outside of the Memory Room, I'm sure would have plenty of advice. I can practically hear his cold-hearted, disembodied voice. "Before the email, you only had suspicion. Nobody had confirmed Mandy's death."

Maybe this place is helping me, even if my coping skills include mimicking an ethereal being trapped in the attic.

Chapter 16

Ethereal Whine

Diesel trucks, several of them this time, stir me from my sleep. It's not even six in the morning yet. Gerald had mentioned he wanted to start from the outside of the house and work his way in. He talked of how odd it was that during the summer, usually high time for construction work, all the major roofing and siding crews in town seemed to have a clear schedule. It works in our favor. Gerald is in a tight time frame.

I glance out my bedroom window. There's a flatbed truck that looks like it has shingles, and there's another truck with a crane on the back. I suppose it's roofing day. Gerald will handle this. I can climb back into bed, put my earbuds in, and listen to some Scandinavian Orchestra until I fall back to sleep. A quick assessment of how I feel leads me to believe I've only had a couple hours of good sleep.

Flicking through my music streaming app, past all the other music I usually listen to, I land on *Holberg*. This is just what I was looking for. I pull my quilt back over myself and adjust the music to a comfortable level. If only I could stay like this forever, at the perfect level of relaxation.

Not even halfway through the first song, a nagging sensation hits deep in my brain. I try to push him away, but he persists. The most prolonged sigh in recorded history accompanies me removing my earbuds and climbing out of bed. Luckily, the work today is outside of the house. Otherwise, I would have to endure the Guardian's whines. Nobody needs to see me first thing in the morning, hair a mess, and the film of sleep still in my eyes.

Gerald is halfway up the stairs from the first floor when I pull the attic ladder down.

"Emmy! Where you going?" he asks.

"I'm going to read. I don't think I'll be able to sleep with all the work going on."

"Alright. Hope you got a good book. They'll be here til three." He says.

The other day, I came up to read, and he shut the hatch. I don't know why he did. He never comes upstairs except to use the restroom. Even if he tried to get to my room to speak to me, there was plenty of space to get around the ladder. The door opens from within the attic, too, but I thought the ladder would fly off the mount when I lost grip on it.

The Guardian seems to know I'm answering his call because the nagging has ceased. Once I'm in the Memory Room, he wastes no time letting me have it.

There are strangers… interlopers.

"They're putting a new roof on the house," I whisper, hoping Gerald is out of earshot.

Why? Why does the house need a new roof?

"Because the one on there is ancient, and we're renovating the whole house."

I told you to keep this room a secret. First, you have your brother living here, and now a whole crew of strangers are crawling around like ants.

"I have this room disguised from Gerald. He thinks

it's just a reading corner. The crew today isn't even going to be in here. This work is getting done with or without your permission. This is my house. You only control this room."

I can make your home very unpleasant to stay in.

"But then, who'll help you find out what happened to you? I don't know how you'll handle tomorrow when they're replacing all the windows in the house."

This is a trespass.

"Nobody is going to bother you so I suggest you not bother me, either."

When are you going to use the locket again? It's been almost a week now.

"I'll be up tonight."

Silence. Just what I wanted.

Chapter 17

Beatrice Taylor

The locket's cold metal sits against the dry skin on my palm as I close my eyes and surrender to its pull. I feel too weak to resist the locket anymore. I intended to abstain from the Memory Room for all of Gerald's stay, yet here I am, only four days after he took residence on my couch. The world around me fades, replaced by the sights and sounds of a different era. I stand on cobblestone streets, surrounded by Victorian London. I'm not Emma anymore—I'm Beatrice, a woman living a simple lifestyle while pining for more.

My attire is plain, reflecting the era's fashion and my low status as a household servant. The dim glow of gas lamps cast an amber hue on the streets, and I make my way with a sense of purpose. The memory within the locket unfolds before me, and I recall the stolen trinket nestled within my handbag—a treasure taken from my employer that holds my future in its delicate form.

The small bauble adorned the mansion of a wealthy banker just an hour before it was liberated in the deft clutches of my thieving hands. It was an evening of grandeur, a soiree where masked faces reveled in decadence. The opportunity was too irresistible for restraint. The memory echoes with the clandestine thrill of slipping the precious trinket into the secret refuge behind my apron's strap, the fabric of my modest work uniform whispering promises of ill-gotten gains. The pulse of stolen riches quickened my blood.

Now, I stand on a secluded street corner. At the edge of the lamplight is a mist of shadows, the same shadows that appear in each of these locket visions. The shadows disperse like incense smoke in a ceiling fan, revealing a man who bears an uncanny resemblance to Cedric Renaud. His dark eyes hold a mysterious allure, and his presence ignites a spark of both familiarity and caution within me.

I cannot dismiss the uncanny resemblance between him and Cedric—their shared carriage, the elusive secret tucked within their gazes. It's as though the mystic force of the locket has orchestrated a meeting with destiny. Yet, rationality resists. This figure cannot be Cedric, for we stand nearly two centuries in the past. The palpable convergence of familiar traits in this historical setting creates a perplexing scene, a dance between recognition and the implausibility of temporal bounds.

I reveal my handbag, unveiling the pilfered trinket cradled within. Bathed in lamplight, it sparkles, its allure a vivid contrast to the ephemeral shadows enveloping us. His lips curl into a smile, sending a shiver down my spine. The stolen relic becomes a centerpiece, a radiant focal point amidst the interplay of light and darkness in this clandestine encounter.

I watch as the man disappears into the London fog, the stolen trinket now in his possession. A sense of both relief and anticipation fills me. With this transaction, I've secured the wealth to buy myself a better life and a higher status. I won't be held down any more, not by anyone. I can flee to a small village and buy myself a sizable estate. I can live the rest of my days in noble splendor.

With a deep breath, I return to the present, the locket's weight anchored against my chest. The memory of Beatrice's act lingers. She was willing to steal to get ahead. Her act changed her life and affected the lives of others. The locket she stole may not have made it into the hands of Amelia Evans or been locked away in the loft of this house, waiting for me.

There's still the question of the man in the vision. Who was he? Why did he pay Beatrice to steal the locket? Was he actually Cedric? The locket loves to give me pieces, never the whole picture, which leaves me thirsting for answers stretching across eons.

The man's presence continues to haunt my thoughts. I click the locket open again, begging for further exploration and elaboration. Against my expectation, the locket obliges my zeal for answers. Moments before the trinket's theft, I'm immersed in the grandeur of the aristocrat's home. The lavish decorations, the elaborate gowns—the atmosphere teemed with strategies of appearance and deception. Beatrice's role as a maid granted her access to hidden corners of the mansion, where local politicians do not glance up from their glasses of brandy, gang leaders do not pause their plotting, the wives accompanying the former two parties occasionally utter a half-hearted thank you as I take crumb ridden platters from the tables.

As I delve deeper into Beatrice's world, I uncover the motivations that fueled her actions. The trinket wasn't merely a given target. It was a means to an end, a strategy to secure her future in a world that often disregarded individuals like her. The locket's power has allowed me to experience her calculated risk, to feel the weight of her ambition.

When the farmhouse returns and the locket shuts, the Guardian advises me. *Don't glamorize this antecessor. Beatrice Taylor… thief. The money she was given was… was life-changing. But she died in a gutter… like Poe.*

On that note, I've had enough of this room for tonight.

Chapter 18

Bedridden

My dreamless sleep is interrupted by Gerald's weathered hand on my arm as he shakes me awake.

"Emmy! Hello! I been tryna wake you up for hours."

I sigh and rollover.

"What's the mattah with you? Don't you go back to sleep. That's what you did the last three times I got you up," he says.

"What's the damn rush?" I ask.

"The fuckin' window crew is here!" he yells.

I jolt up, eyes wide. "I thought that was tomorrow."

"Today is tomahrow!"

"Ok, ok. I'll get myself together."

Gerald leaves, closing the door behind him. He puts too much force into shutting the door, and reverberations shoot through the wall. My heart is beating rapidly. Gerald has always had a temper, but I've not been on the wrong side of it in years.

Light floods the room and stings my eyes as I draw the curtains back. I feel like I just crawled out of hell. I go over to the mirror. I look like I just crawled out of hell. I put on a wine-red shirt and blue jeans. While I brush my hair, I wonder the whole time if I'll fall over. The room is spinning.

Alternating between clinging to the railing and leaning against the wall, I go to the bathroom. I splash cold water on my face and press the towel against it for a few seconds. A wave of nausea batters the inside of my skull, and I can barely pull the towel away before I retch into the sink. Yellow bile splashes across the porcelain. I splash more water on my face and towel off again. Nothing comes up this time.

My skin is pale, paler than usual, under my eyes are dark, and my cheeks are flushed in contrast to the rest of my colorless face. It looks like I've been crying. My eyes are glassy and bloodshot. Any minute, a camera crew will show up, and my close friends and family will rise from the grave to tell me I should stop doing drugs.

With shaking hands, I smooth my hair back and exit the bathroom. Pausing at the top of the stairs, I imagine each step's impact, the twisting of my body, the torsion of each vertebra, and the final skid across the floor in the foyer. Instead of throwing myself down the flight of doom, I cling to the handrail like an old lady. Every time I put weight on my leg, my knee balances dangerously on the brink of buckling. My shaking hands no longer glide along the rail. The sweat has seen to that.

Halfway down the steps, I catch myself against the wall. There's a loud thud, and Gerald steps out from the living room. His furrowed brows lift almost to his hairline, and he rushes up the last six steps I intend to descend.

"Christ, you look like shit," Gerald grabs my arm to brace me.

"You should see the other guy," I lean against him. Sometimes, I wonder whether he or Michelangelo's David is denser. Here I am, insulting him in the secrecy of my mind while he is helping me down the stairs and back to my desk chair.

"Just sit here. I'll get you some watah."

I sink against the chair. My trembling hand fumbles to find the levers on the side. There's a pop as the tension in the chair's mechanisms release and I can tilt the seat and back freely. I lean as far back as I can and close my eyes.

Footsteps, the clink of glass against the desk, and something else, something paper. I open my eyes to see a plate of buttered toast. I thank Gerald while he goes to the front door to let the window crew in. He says something to them I can't hear, but it must not have been vital for me to hear because several pairs of work boots scurry up the stairs.

I open my eyes as a solo pair of boots walks back toward my study.

"I'll be upstairs with them. We're gonna be cuttin' off the drywall around the windows. That way, we're not messin' dem up when we tear down the rest of the walls. They're only doing the seven windows upstairs today. Tomahrow, they'll be here to do the six down here."

"Ok," I croak out.

"You got your phone? Just text me if you need anything. Try to drink and get that food down. If you don't feel bettah this aftahnoon, maybe it'll be time to find a doctor."

I nod. Gerald leaves.

Hammers, saws, and loud footsteps lulled me to sleep, or maybe my exhaustion was too intense to be nullified by the racket. A dark and silent sleep brought me five hours forward to when Gerald was shouting his farewells to the crew.

Rubbing the sleep out of my eyes, the still-full glass of water taunts my dry mouth. I drink while I inspect the toast. The butter has faded, turning almost transparent on the surface of the toast. A gnat is stuck, drowned in the vegetable oils they engineer into looking and tasting like butter. The whole house smells of plaster.

Gerald returns to check on me. His face scrunches when he spies the untouched toast and the barely dropped water level of the glass. He stammers through the start of three separate sentences, and then his shoulders lower, "Let's get you back to bed."

I didn't feel as bad on the way back to bed as I did this morning, but still in the running for the worst I've ever felt. Once I climbed under the quilt, I wondered if this was because I was up all night using the locket. Last night was the first time I'd ever used the locket twice in one night. Still, I feel more than tired.

Chapter 19

House of Bones

The following day was a waste. I hardly left my bed and thus accomplished nothing. All of the windows were replaced downstairs. It didn't bother me at all. Gerald brought me water and saltine crackers early in the day and, later on, a couple of slices of pizza. The only drawback to this lifestyle was that I didn't feel tired when night fell, so I wasted most of the night watching movies.

I felt refreshed when I woke up the next day, at almost two o'clock in the afternoon. The house was quiet, so I looked out my new window with the plastic film still adhered to the panes, to see if Gerald was home. I saw that not only my and Gerald's vehicles were in the driveway, but also Cedric's.

I pull myself together, get dressed, and navigate to the bathroom to primp and preen myself to presentability. My neat appearance is in stark contrast to the appearance of the house. All the walls downstairs have been reduced to nothing more than two by fours. I can see my two guests in the living room. Cedric is sweating, hands covered in plaster, his suit jacket draped on the back of the couch. He's in a pretty conservatively colored suit for once, Gray tweed with a black shirt. If not for the plaster smudged across his hips, I would say it's the nicest ensemble I've seen him in.

Gerald's chuckling at something as I walk into the living room. He didn't notice me until Cedric glanced toward the door while Gerald was in the middle of a joke. He didn't finish the joke after "then there was dis one time she–" and whipped around to look at me.

"You just wakin' up?"

"Yeah."

"How'd you sleep through all this?" He gestures around the room. His question likely didn't require an answer, but I shrug anyway.

"Are you feeling better today, Miss Emma?"

"A lot better," I say, forcing the corners of my mouth upwards. I have to maintain appearances.

Glancing around, I see all the drywall and laths are already out of the house, no doubt in the dumpster. "Do you need help with anything?"

"Nah," Gerald says, "We got all the wahk done foh the day. You and I need to talk about the siding. The stuff on there is cedah, and nobody carries it anymore, so it's gonna have to change."

"What are the options?" I ask.

"I always recommend vinyl."

"Do they make vinyl that looks like wood?"

One of Gerald's brows raises slightly, and his eyes dart. "I'll have to see."

"I've seen a house with wood vinyl before, when I was in Vermont last summer," Cedric pipes in. "The owner said it was a bit pricey, though."

"Well, nawthing but the best for Emmy."

I sigh slightly. Hopefully, Cedric doesn't pick up the "Emmy" thing. Paired with the "Miss," I'll feel like a kindergarten teacher.

Chapter 20

Mysticism, and Baseball

It dawned on me that Gerald and Cedric had never met before today. This day of work with just the two of them couldn't have been planned. Gerald likely was working alone, and Cedric swung by for something else entirely, and Gerald drafted him into helping out. Cedric didn't have to say yes. I have to make his lost day up to him.

"Hey," I get their attention, "How about I take you two out for dinner as a 'thank you' for all the hard work today."

"That sounds amazing," Cedric says, the gap in his teeth beaming at me.

Gerald's cheeks and eyebrows seem keen on meeting, "You hate going out."

"I'm getting better," I say, the tone coming off more defensive than I intended. "Plus, I've been cooped up for the last few days."

"Where you wanna go?" Gerald asks.

"I don't know. I haven't been anywhere in town yet, so I'm up for suggestions."

"You said you been here awhile," Gerald says to

Cedric. "There a sports bar? Game's on tonight, and I could go for some beers."

Cedric pauses briefly, "There is one right off Main Street, on Kashe Avenue."

Before Cedric had finished his sentence, Gerald's car keys clambered as he snatched them from the window sill. "Alright, Emmy can ride with me, and we'll follow you there."

I agree with the plan, even though I would rather drive myself. Gerald's truck always smells like American cheese from fast food burgers.

***

We lost Cedric along the way, but it wasn't hard to find this place. The International Space Station crew probably spends their downtime wondering what it would be like to finally go to *The Game Time Tavern*.

Gerald made sure to sit between Cedric and me. Whether he did it to irritate me or hang out with his new friend, I don't know. I haven't sat at a bar since college, but I was instantly reminded why you shouldn't go with a group above two people.

When it was time to order our drinks, I got a Coke. Cedric and Gerald ordered the same beer on draft in unison, and upon realizing they shared a go-to drink, they fist-bumped in a way that made me physically recoil.

Maine doesn't have a baseball team, but judging by the Red Sox memorabilia on the wall, this place will be friendly to my loudmouth brother. I used to never understand why there would be riots in some cities if the home team lost, but then Gerald spent a weekend in jail after the Sox lost a game. This was before he married and allegedly "calmed down," though.

Gerald's team is winning, so he doesn't want to miss any action. After two beers, he taps his leg restlessly against the bar, waiting for a commercial break. He wasn't the only one waiting, for as soon as Gerald left the bar, Cedric struck up a conversation with me.

"Miss Emma, not long ago, maybe a decade, being able to enjoy American life, share a beer with friends, I would have thought impossible."

I wasn't sure how to reply, but he continued without my reply.

"I did well in school, and I got to study abroad. I went to England. When I was there, I found love for the unapologetic lifestyle of the West. But I learned something else, too. I was fascinated with occultism."

"Occultism? Like secret societies and magic?"

"Yes, but so much of it is just men's clubs, somewhere we can go to be alone and not have to hold ourselves back from our true self-expression."

"Do you believe in the supernatural?" I ask. "I've had some brushes with things I can't explain."

"Of course. It's an old house."

Gerald sat down before the conversation could carry further. Cedric and I never got a chance to speak more. He left without warning.

Ethan McGrane

Chapter 21

Aya

Eyes closed, inhale quickly, exhale slowly, click the locket, open eyes, surrender to its pull. The world around me shifts and transforms. I'm no longer Emma. I'm Aya, an artisan in ancient Egypt. Memories flood into my mind of a life spent amidst the grandeur of a civilization reverent to its gods.

The sand reflects the sun's light and heat, casting long shadows in the temple's entryway and turning the structure into a furnace. Chisels against stone drown out all other sounds. I oversee this temple's adornment the final decorations after the masons have constructed it. This honor and responsibility intertwines my fate with the gods themselves.

My hand reaches up to the beads strung across my collarbones. The necklace's center is a piece of blueish metal, and my fingers run along its near-reflective surface. My vision shimmers and the illusion feels near collapse. Some artisans seem to move in reverse, and my breathing feels wrong. Once Aya has ceased the admiration of her amulet, things return to normal, with a sense of nausea lingering.

The temple's walls, once completed, will have not one

square inch free of the intricate hieroglyphics telling the stories of our people, the secrets of the cosmos, and the connection between the divine and mortal realms. Among these carvings, one god reigns supreme— the deity who gifted souls to humanity, Ra, allowing us the privilege of reincarnation. It is a bond of eternal gratitude, one driving me to ensure every detail of this temple is perfect. Every chisel strikes against the stone with purpose. Each artisan contributes to the collective offering of devotion to the gods. The temple's construction isn't a simple erecting of walls. It's an expression of gratitude to the beings responsible for our existence.

Amidst the colonnades, my fingers weave a dance, caressing the curves and angles of the symbols etched into the stone. These aren't mere images but a testament to our communion with the divine, an arcane language spoken by gods and deciphered by mortals. Each hieroglyph transcends simplicity, acting as a mystical bridge between realms. Countless years have been dedicated to unraveling their secrets, delving into the ancient tapestry that binds our world to the cosmic unknown. I've spent my life learning these symbols.

In the heart of the temple, the altar awaits, a sacred space where offerings will be made and prayers will be chanted. It is a nexus where our souls are bound by threads woven through time. Lamplight dances on the polished stones. If the gods are the sun, we are the oil lamps— an imitation. The aroma of incense wafts through the air, mingling with fresh sand and stone scents. It's a sensory symphony. I pause for a moment to appreciate the vision brought to life.

The wall behind the altar is adorned with a mural, stretching thirty feet from floor to ceiling and sixty feet from one side of the temple to the next. A tunnel entrance sits in the middle of the mural. It once was the entryway to a tomb.

Priests lay resting in the catacomb. Have their souls already returned to join the living once more? Perhaps I am one of them.

I grab a lamp and start down the hall to the tomb, wanting to take some time to reflect on today's work. More hieroglyphs and paintings line this hallway. I am not responsible for these ones. When this tomb was built decades before my birth, artisans like me decorated this hall. I pause to read one of the inscriptions, and the ceiling before me collapses. Large pieces of stone slam into the ground. Dust and sand are flung into my face.

Coughing violently, grasping at my eyes from the pain, the lamb shatters against the ground, and flames erupt. The air thickens from the smoke. The coughing exacerbates. I step backward to get away from the hazards. My fellow artisans rally to the mouth of the tomb, but none enter to save me.

Pull yourself together.

I'm coughing too much to reply.

He's going to find out about this room.

With each cough, the shadows around my vision increase.

Stop it. It was only a vision. Nothing more than a dream.

Between my hacking, I hear heavy footsteps on the stairs.

I'll fix this myself, then.

The reading light on the table beside me illuminates, a book opens, and the locket flies out of my hands. I can't breathe. I still feel the heat from the oil lamp, the dust and sand pouring into my airways. I cough more, and the black fills my entire vision.

Chapter 22

"We don't know what's wrong with you"

The initial whisper of life comes olfactorily—the air, a blend more of disinfectant than oxygen, assaults my senses. My eyes flutter open to confirm my suspicion—a hospital room, the sterile environment accentuated by the harsh fluorescence penetrating closed blinds. Despite their effort, darkness looms within, only to be tinged orange by the distant glow of street lamps filtering through the window.

There's a peculiar solace in the hospital. In this haven of healing, the reins of control slip from my grasp. No need to heed the Guardian's call, worry about my soul's temporal journey, or whose thoughts I'll inhabit. There are no truths to unravel. Here, I recline, eyes fixed on the flickering TV, a respite dedicated to recuperation from the tumult of recent events.

The Guardian told me nothing could hurt me while I use the locket. Even if my antecessor died, I would wake up in the Memory Room. So, what happened? Why did I continue to feel the sand in my eyes, nasal passage, throat, and lungs? Between the exhaustion and my recent episode, I think the Guardian has misled me.

I push it all out of my mind. I don't want to waste this opportunity to ignore my preoccupations. Turning my attention to the television, I see a true crime documentary in full swing. Southern Colorado, in the summer of 1992, a deputy conducting a routine traffic stop shoots the driver and discovers two dead women in the back of the truck. The next day, a gang hit squad went after him.

Before I can fully engross myself in the documentary, Gerald looks over at me and then presses the nurse call button. The nurse promptly enters the room with a squeak of her sneakers, reads the machines I'm hooked up to, and then says she'll get a doctor in as soon as possible.

Gerald doesn't initiate a conversation, so I try to get back to the TV. I've lost my place, so none of it makes sense now. I flip through some channels. The nightly news, late-night cartoons, and a sketch comedy show were boring. I land on a baking show. It's not something I would typically watch, but at this point, I've already switched from trying to relax to mindlessly passing the time until the doctor returns.

My brother snores through the baking show, the following challenge show where four people have to cook with ingredients I've never heard of, and the cooking theory show about what temperature to cook your cut of cow to. A nurse breezes through the room, flicks my IV a few times, and says she prefers rare and won't eat anything over medium.

The hospital brings back unwelcome memories. Nurses, despite their place of work, remain strangers, and my aversion to the unfamiliar resurfaces. In a space I attempt to claim as my own, incessant intrusions from these unfamiliar faces leave me unsettled and ill at ease.

As the cooking channel changes to a breakfast-oriented program, I notice the window blinds are getting a light blue tint. The morning is almost here.

ASAP turned out to be over two hours. The doctor

entered with a flip of the light switch. Gerald stirs, and the doctor introduces herself as Dr. Mitchell. She flips through some papers in her folder and then looks at me.

"Well, good news– the tests all came back in the normal range, and you tested negative for cold, flu, strep, and all the other cough-related illnesses."

"Ahright," Gerald says.

I remain silent, my way of inviting the doctor to continue.

"So, your brother said you had a recent spell and couldn't get out of bed or really move around on your own for a couple of days. Since you recently relocated from Boston, and you also being underweight by a little over twenty pounds, there's a chance your symptoms are brought on by a combination of stress and lifestyle factors."

I bite the inside of my cheek so I don't say anything cruel and ill-advised.

Dr. Mitchell's mouth twitches to the side, and she looks down, doing the same thing Old Man Henry did before rushing me out of his house. She flips through pages without any sense of purpose, not settling on any of them long enough to read anything, and then returns her gaze to me.

"Well, I'm going to refer you to a therapist. She sees a lot of my patients. I hear she's the best. We have your current address, so we'll mail you the bill. I'll send a nurse in here to get the machines off you and your IV out, and then you'll be free to go."

"Thanks, dahc," Gerald says. I nod, and Dr. Mitchell leaves.

I didn't have to wait two hours for the following medical professional to arrive. They weren't the same nurse as last time, but he quickly peeled off the electrodes and removed the IV. I always thought the aftercare for a needle being removed from an artery funny, if not optimistic. A piece of medical tape and a cotton ball will prevent anything from entering through the portal liters of fluids took.

Gerald, thoughtful as ever, brought one of my hoodies along. I pull that on over my pajamas. As my bare feet dangle above the linoleum, I ask if he brought a pair of my shoes. He did not. But the pharmacy on the ground floor sells flip-flops, so he got me a pair he thought would fit. Is there a more uncomfortable feeling than leaving a hospital, half-dressed in a mismatched get-up, wearing cheap flip-flops two sizes too large? Well, probably choking on non-existent sand from thousands of years, an ocean and a continent away may be up there. Still, as Jean-Paul Sartre penned, "Hell is other people," so I'm in Hell every time we pass somebody, regardless of whether they wear scrubs, a hospital gown, a police uniform, or everyday casual wear.

Chapter 23

The Theosite

I kick the flip-flops off to the corner between the foyer and the dining room. The lightweight fabric of my tank top is clinging to the fleece lining of my sweatshirt, and it feels weird, but I'll put up with it for now. I'm not tired, so I may well start my day.

The first order of business is to set my coffee to brew and then start my laptop across the hall. I'll take the morning slow, relax in my office chair, clear my email inbox, and decide what's next.

A ringing similar to tinnitus resounds in both of my ears. Before I carry out my morning routine, I should go to the attic to see what the Guardian wants. It is odd how clear his voice is when I'm in the attic, but it may as well be a dog whistle down here. In my mind, I think of the reasons I can't go to the attic right now, but the ringing continues.

A knock at the front door terminates the ringing. Of course, I'm the only person without plans for my time today. Through the wooden skeleton of the first floor, I spy Gerald answering the door. Hopefully, it's just a contractor or deliveryman dropping off materials for Gerald's next big project. I'm not in the mood for visitors.

I don't need to see his face to know who's wearing the salmon-colored suit with a lime green shirt. I run my hands through my hair, smoothing it back.

"Good morning, Miss Emma," Cedric pulls the chair in the corner up to the desk and sits down.

"Good morning," I sit up in my desk chair.

"You are feeling better?" Cedric points to my right wrist, where the hospital bracelets are.

"Yes, all better."

"Look, I came here today because I need to talk to you."

Here I thought he just needed to borrow a cup of flour.

He continues, "I'm not a New England Chroniclers Society member. I'm a member of the Theosian Order."

I raise an eyebrow, "Never heard of it."

"We're an order founded by the great mysticist Aldric Crosby nearly a hundred years ago. My line of work for the order is the acquisition and study of supernatural items. Items such as the locket in your attic."

"Get out."

Cedric's eyes widen. His left hand tightens around the arm of the chair. "Miss Emma…"

"Get out!"

Cedric starts to speak again, but this time, Gerald's hand clasps the back of the chair, and he says, "Hey bud, she told you to leave. You should leave. Let her cool off."

He does not immediately heed Gerald and looks back toward me, but my brother pats him on the shoulder, causing him to jump. Gerald escorts him out, and I sink back into my chair. Cedric knew about the locket the whole time. He let me lie to him about it. He saw for his own eyes the lengths the Guardian would go just to hide it.

After dinner last night, I thought I could call Cedric a

friend. Now… well, now I have to reevaluate our relationship. What do I know for sure about him? Not much. The only thing I can say for sure is that he has a strange affinity for vibrant suits.

Ethan McGrane

Ethan McGrane

Chapter 24

Isolde Kovacs

I resolved to have a few days of rest. I made it through three days without the locket, a new record. But I can no longer hold back. I tried to distract myself. I used to be able to tune everything out and retreat into my work. Numbers make sense to me, but they aren't helping me make sense of anything now. I helped Gerald hang some drywall, mostly just holding the sheets while he screwed them into the studs. I got him a TV so he doesn't have to sit on his phone during his free time. I try to watch it, but I can't focus on anything. The locket and the endless wealth of knowledge it holds are too enticing.

Eyes closed, inhale quickly, exhale slowly, click the locket, open eyes, and surrender to its pull. I'm no longer Emma. I am Isolde Kovacs, a thief in Renaissance-era Krakow, Poland.

The night air is crisp in the shadows. My heart races with anticipation. The moonlight dances on the cobblestones, casting silver to paint the otherwise plain stone city in ethereal light. I adjust the black mask concealing my identity, reminding myself I am a ghost, a phantom with purpose.

My target gleams like a siren's call from across the street. The Bank of Krakow. Ornate architecture and fortified walls have earned a reputation as impenetrable. I thrive on challenges. With a final glance around to ensure I'm unseen, I step into the shadows to maneuver undetected toward the bank's service entrance.

The security is formidable, testifying to the wealth and secrets it guards. Guards patrol the perimeter, footsteps echoing against the cobblestones. I crouch low, syncing my heartbeat with their movements so I can time my approach with precision. A soft breeze rustles the leaves, masking the sound of my footsteps as I slip through a guard's blind spot.

My fingers brush against the cool metal of my tools. My lockpicks have never failed me. I kneel before the bank's imposing entrance, my nimble fingers working deftly as I navigate the intricate mechanisms. The lock yields to my touch, the sound barely a whisper in the night. The door opens just wide enough for me to slip inside. I ease the door closed behind me.

The bank's interior is dimly lit, the flicker of candlelight casting elongated shadows that dance upon the marble floors. My steps are light, and my movements are deliberate as I navigate the maze of corridors. A heist is a symphony of strategy, every action calculated to avoid detection. Thanks to my childhood friend working as a clerk here, I move with the confidence of someone who's studied every inch of the bank's layout.

Finally, I arrive at the heart of the bank—the vault. Its massive door stands before me, an imposing barrier between me and my prize. But I'm prepared. My tools make quick work of the vault's locking mechanism, each click a triumph piercing the silence of the night. The door swings open, revealing row upon row of treasures, jewels, artifacts, and gold.

I'm not to worry about anything aside from my

objective. My employer will give me all the gold and jewels I want, enough to retire from this odious occupation. My gaze singles out lockbox forty-two, containing one thing: a locket. It glows softly in the dim light, a beacon of mystery and power.

I was instructed to only take the locket and not open it under any circumstance. Its disappearance may go unnoticed for several years. If I get greedy and take too much, the city will be alert.

As I wrap the locket in cloth and place it in my belt bag, I feel a rush of triumph and exhilaration. So long as I make it out undetected, this heist is a success, a masterpiece of strategy and skill. But there's something else. The locket airs of curiosity. It beckons me, but I must resist until I am away from this bank.

With my objective secured, I retreat from the vault and retrace my steps through the bank. The guards remain oblivious to my presence. Their vigilance is no match for my prowess as a thief. The night air greets me once more as I step out onto the cobblestones, the locket safely in my possession.

I slip back into the shadows, making my way through the streets of Krakow with the locket as my prize. The city sleeps, unaware of the heist that has transpired. With each step, I put distance between myself and death. Indeed, were I to be caught, I would swing from the gallows in the central square. I unmask myself. Now, I'm just an ordinary woman walking home. A wall of shadows obscures the rest of the street, but I enter them and return to the Oak Cove House.

The locket's energy courses through me as I sit in the present. In the span of moments, I've experienced the rush of the Renaissance, the heartbeat of Krakow, and the triumph of a successful strategy.

Another thief in your line. I may reconsider allowing you unfettered access to this sanctuary.

"I'm no thief."

With a splitting headache, I return to my room on the second floor and climb into bed.

Chapter 25

Dr. Calloway

"Remember, Emmy, you're payin' them for an hour. Use the full hour," Gerald says.

"I will, I will," I say.

Closing the door to his truck, I wonder if he's compelling me to use the entire hour because he's considerate of my well-being or if he wants more time at the hardware store. I argued with him for so long that I was five minutes late for my appointment. "The doctor said to take it easy," Gerald had said. "Driving is easy," I argued to no avail.

This place looks more like I would find The Unabomber, not the highest-regarded mental health professional in South Thornbrook. It's a small house right on the water. The security camera facing the driveway, undecorated gazebo, empty jacuzzi, and pine nettle-covered car makes me think I may be more well-adjusted than this doctor.

Therapists have never done me any good. I don't think this one will, either. I've always had my lion's share of problems. Just before I reach the door, I realize Gerald dropped me off today because he knows me. I have a history of avoidant behavior. He wanted to ensure I saw this therapist today instead of going to the diner for an hour.

I'm not as bad as I used to be. The sign on the door, *Office of Dr. S. Calloway M.D. – please come in*, ushers me to what appears to be the doctor's living room. Typically, when I go somewhere new, my heart rushes out of unfamiliarity, but I've been to many unfamiliar places in the last couple of weeks. Moreover, I've been to foreign periods and spoken exotic languages. I've been myself and not myself at the same time. I remember the dream about being institutionalized. Maybe I should leave out everything about the locket, the Memory Room, and its Guardian.

Before I sit in the "waiting room," the good doctor whisks me into her office. Stepping into her office is like stepping into a different building altogether. The waiting room had a rustic, late 90's feel between the old furniture and wood panel walls. In contrast, the office has pristine white walls, abstract paintings, and a couple of house plants. The light gray, textureless linoleum floor has a coffee table in the middle of it, with two wine-red leather sofas facing each other across the table.

She sits on the sofa on the far side of the coffee table, and I sit on the one closer. She sits back and crosses her legs. I fold my hands in my lap, but I can't bring myself to lean back into the couch and relax.

"So," Dr. Calloway starts, "You were referred to me by Dr. Mitchell at Thornbrook Regional. Can you tell me what she referred you for?"

"I've been having recent health issues. Dr. Mitchell thinks they are brought on by behavioral or psychosomatic issues."

"Do you have a history of such things?"

"No, I'm usually so healthy I have a hard time justifying how much of my salary goes to health insurance.

Since I've moved here from Boston, I've been struggling."

"Moving can be stressful. Was this move planned for a while beforehand?"

"It was more a spur of the moment. My best friend had just passed away. I took a road trip to get away from everything, and I bought a house here after stopping for gas."

"Sometimes grief, or avoiding grief, can lead us to act impulsively. Still, it's quite a jump from buying gas to buying a house."

"I can't explain why. I overheard a couple people talking about whether the house would ever sell, that it had been on the market for too long and likely needed a lot of work."

"The work required to fix it was actually a selling point for you?" Dr. Calloway takes a sip from her water bottle.

"I wanted a distraction. I wanted something I could put all my effort into."

"Past tense. You no longer feel like the house is giving you that distraction?"

"I don't know how to fix a house. I had to bring my brother up so he could basically do all the work."

"So, the house isn't the distraction you hoped for. Do you have anything else going on? Any other ways to distract yourself?"

"I was able to bring my work with me, remote work, you know."

"I'm familiar with the concept."

"Anyway, I thought distracting yourself from your feelings was bad?" I ask.

"It's not always a bad thing. Sometimes, the only thing that can heal certain emotional injuries is time and distance. You've put distance between yourself and your tragedy. Now, you need time to heal." Dr. Calloway sits her notepad down, takes a sip from her glass of water, and then asks, "Have you made any friends since you moved to South Thornbrook?"

"I made one but found out he was lying to me."

"Is it something you can forgive him for?"

I hadn't thought about whether or not to forgive Cedric yet. He lied to me the whole time I knew him, but I always knew he was more than he let on, what with the colorful suits, the symbol on his lighter… He's an oddity, and I shouldn't have been surprised. He trusted me enough to tell me the truth, and I told him to leave.

Dr. Calloway interrupts my cycle of reflection. "Whatever he did, if you decide you can forgive him, I recommend you do. You won't heal and move on if you don't fully embrace your new life in South Thornbrook."

Chapter 26

Reconciliation

I park my BMW between a beat-up Toyota Corolla and an old Ford pickup. This is the place Cedric told me about, the bar right across the street from his motel. Rusty's, where the establishment's name matches the cars in front of it.

Scanning the room reveals tables occupied by what appears to be a clone of one man wearing different colored t-shirts and haircuts. However, Cedric is easy to pick out, as he dresses like his color palette was selected by people he lost a bet with. The lemon collar of his shirt is poking up above the red plaid of his jacket as he hunches over the bar.

He's sitting at the corner of the bar. While it's lucky for me, I can't help but wonder if it's intentional the two stools to his left are vacant while the rest of the place seems packed.

I put a hand on his shoulder to get his attention. "I thought I might find you here."

Cedric looks from his drink to me. His eyes are glassy, his eyelids resting lower than usual, and blood vessels showing through his corneas.

"Miss Emma! I wasn't sure I'd see you so soon," He

slurs over every "s" in the sentence.

I sit down next to him as he waves the bartender over. Holding up his glass, he requests, "One of these for her, and a water for me, please."

"What is that?" I point to his glass, with two tiny slivers of an ice cube sliding erratically along the bottom.

"A Rusty Nail," he answers.

It doesn't sound very appetizing. "Is that this place's signature?"

"Why, because of the name?"

"Yeah, is this place called Rusty's because of the drink?"

"No, it's named after the owner, Mr. Russell."

A glass of ice water finds the coaster in front of Cedric, and a highball glass that looks like whiskey on rocks with an orange slice stops the coaster from sliding across the bar in front of me.

"I really don't think this is my kind of drink," I say.

"Have you ever had one before?"

"No."

"Try it. I think you will find it perfect for you."

Hesitantly, I raise the glass to my lips and take a small sip. The gasoline taste and burn I was expecting hit, but beyond that, smooth flavor notes flooded in. I can't nail down all the notes, but I'm reminded of candles burning while trying to get through a good book, smokiness, and... honey?

"See, I knew you would like it," Cedric says after I take a second sip.

"I'm sorry about the other day."

"As am I. I should have given you more time to unwind from the hospital. But there are some things it is imperative you know about the locket."

I glance over my shoulder.

"Don't worry about the crowd. I find if you talk about

extraordinary things casually, most people tune it out."

I nod for him to continue.

"The locket– you need to be careful with it. You can't use it too often."

"Why?" I ask.

"Magical items, such as the locket, require energy. Energy can be stored in certain crystals and gemstones, but if the object is without such accessories, by using them, you become the power source."

"So, that's why I've felt so tired all the time?"

"It goes far beyond feeling tired. It can sap all of your life force and kill you."

I look into my drink. I've never really enjoyed life, but I don't want to die.

"How often should I use the locket?"

"Make sure you feel well rested, don't use it if you already feel tired, and definitely do not use it more than once a night."

We both take sips of our drink.

"How do you know so much about the locket?"

"It used to be in the possession of the Theosian Order."

"Then, how did it end up in my attic?"

Chapter 27

Sigurd Slodi

Cedric's counsel echoes in my thoughts. The power within the locket is both a boon and a peril. I recognize its allure, its ability to transport me to realms beyond the veil of the present. However, my newfound understanding unveils the treacherous currents beneath its mesmerizing surface. The Guardian, a shadowy figure with hidden motives, lurks in the periphery. Trusting either blindly would be as reckless as sleeping in an untethered raft on unfamiliar waters. Yet, armed with Cedric's guidance, I find myself at the crossroads of caution and curiosity. I now have power — the power to wield the Memory Room judiciously, to tread the corridors of time with a measured step.

The risks, once nebulous and ominous, now stand revealed. Armed with this awareness, the Memory Room beckons. I possess wisdom earned through peril and step into its confines with the newfound confidence of a warrior who knows the lay of the battlefield. The dance with time becomes a calculated duet, the cadence of my steps attuned to the subtle rhythms of the locket's arcane magic.

Before opening the locket, I gaze through the

window. The stars are especially dazzling tonight. I love living near the water, far enough from a population dense enough to blot out the stars with artificial lights.

I have the privilege of reliving a night from over a thousand years ago. Tiny dots of light scatter throughout the night, but they aren't stars. Torches glow dimly along the sides of small wooden huts, water laps along the hull of my ship, and waves caress the shoreline. I hope the waves are enough to disguise, from my soon-to-be victims, the sound of wood creaking.

I've been patrolling the coast for almost a week now. I, Sigurd Haraldsson, called *Sloði* by my peers, meaning "good for nothing," will lead a raid so successful it will change my fame. The air is charged with anticipation, a palpable energy humming through our veins. We descend upon this foreign land tonight to claim its riches and etch our names into history.

The settlers here will never see us coming. They are in their hall, celebrating a recent victory over their neighboring clan. They will have spoils from their forays. They won't be at full strength between the drinking and their fresh wounds.

Undetected up to this point, we breach the entrance of the hall. Chaos erupts in a clash of swords as all the men spring to action while the women and children scramble to the exit at the back of the hall. Their flimsy shields falter against our storm of blades. I'm a wraith amidst the pandemonium, moving with precision. Amidst the clash of steel and the primal roars of combat, my eyes lock onto a sword hanging on the wall over the throne. The steel of the pommel embraces a highly reflective piece of blue-hued metal. It calls to me with irresistible allure. The mysterious metal within its pommel. Its aura feels just like the locket.

Suddenly, amidst the fray, the Frisian chieftain emerges, his massive silhouette cutting through the smoke and turmoil. "Viking!" the chieftain bellows, a challenge thrown into the tumult of the skirmish. The title, shouted as a slur, echoes across the battlefield, a harbinger of impending confrontation. The chieftain pulls the sword with the strange pommel from the wall and shouts to me as he catches sight of my mantling onto the feast table. I step over a dead man strewn across a platter of roasted beast. My leather shoe smears the fringe of a corpse's blood pool, causing my right foot to slide briefly. I regain my footing and raise my sword. In my hand, it is a perfectly balanced instrument of death.

The dance of blades, a lethal choreography, begins. I, agile and relentless, weave through the chieftain's strikes, his sword moving akin to a felled tree. My opponent is a force of raw power, swinging his broadsword with primal fury, each blow aimed to crush bone and sever sinew. The clash of steel reverberates through the hall, a discordant melody of life and death. In the heart of the chaos, the chieftain and I remain engaged in deadly combat, our swords tracing arcs of steel in the firelight. Sigurd's agility counters the chieftain's strength, their blades a testament to the clash of two titans. Sparks dance as the swords meet, and with every parry and strike, the night bears witness to a deadly ballet, a symphony of violence.

After grueling minutes, minutes that stretch to an eternity, the chieftain and I are the only combatants remaining. My raiders have overpowered the Frisian clan. Muffled shouts from the rest of the village penetrate the hall as my men plunder the households. Several of my Vikings remain in the hall, shouting and cheering me on as I clash with the brute chieftain.

The chieftain swings his sword with increasing exhaustion. His breath rasps from his open mouth. Sweat pours from his hairline. When he recovers from one strike to the next, his hands shake. His legs no longer appear to be sufficient to hold him against us invaders.

Like a matador, I sense my opponent is ready to be dispatched deliberately. He raises his sword overhead and brings it down with a final wind fury that catches me off guard. I parry it with my shield, a large piece of my defense splintering off, flying through the air. The chieftain slashes his sword sideways. I step back in time for the point to narrowly miss my throat.

Off balance from his last flurry, I stab my sword sideways under his left rib. I follow through with the motion until the chieftain's side butts against the cross guard above the handle. The chieftain stumbles backward, dropping his sword against the wooden floor with a deafening clatter.

My Vikings cheer louder as they realize our victory. The chieftain begins pulling my sword from his side, recoiling in pain as the reddened steel emerges from his flesh. He doesn't manage to pull the blade too far. His arm spasms as his body convulses. He coughs, blood sputtering through his mustache, dripping down into his gray beard. He sinks back into his throne, eyes wide open though the life has since left them. The man can keep his throne. He can keep my sword, too. Of this conquest, I only wanted fame, to lead a successful raid, but the broadsword sitting on the ground before me, its allure is far greater than improving my reputation. It must be mine.

As my fingers graze the reflective metal within the pommel, a lightning bolt courses through me, connecting the past with the present. I feel the illusion break. Sigurd's adrenaline wanes, his heart goes from a rapid pace to an uneven one, and his breathing starts to rasp. He looks from his hand clasped around the sword handle up his arm, disappearing into his tattered grey tunic. He knows something isn't right, but his thirst for victory and glory takes over, and he returns to his battle-heightened state.

The reflective metal within the sword's pommel continues to emanate with the same energy as the locket. The memory of Sigurd the Good-for-Nothing and his raid gradually fade, leaving me standing amidst the aftermath of battle. The connection between the metal and the locket remains a bridge between eras, a reminder of the binding across time.

As I return to the present, I continue to feel the sword's weight in my hand, the resonance of the reflective metal still coursing through my being. The battle may be over, but the echoes of the past linger.

The locket delves into the distant past. Unnecessary. The Guardian's voice shatters my reflection on the recent vision, bringing me fully to the present.

"I can't control what it shows me. Besides, I need to understand you and your predicament," I try to reason.

It doesn't seem to be the locket's concern.

"It's part of this, part of you."

Superfluous history.

"There might be clues and answers in these visions."

Answers lie elsewhere.

"How can you be so sure? No matter how far past, I won't ignore anything the locket shows me."

Folly. Seek the present.

"If I can't understand the locket, how can I help you?"

The locket clouds your judgment and draws your attention away from the answers.

"I can't let go of a potential solution."

Solutions are elsewhere. Focus.

"The locket might hold the key."

The key is not in "its" history.

"I won't abandon any lead."

Stubbornness hinders. Look elsewhere. The locket shows you ancient history. My answers lie in recent history.

I give up on arguing with him. He's in a sour mood. I can't seem to convince him. I have things to do early in the morning, anyway, and that's only three hours away.

Ethan McGrane

morning, anyway, and that's only three hours away.

Chapter 28

"Not leaving you here alone"

Ninety percent of my worldly possessions have been pushed into the middle of my bedroom and covered with a plastic sheet. It was Gerald's idea to cover them up. Lately, I've been caring less and less about material things. All morning, I've been helping my brother essentially demolish this room. I'm sore from all the trips up and down the stairs carrying drywall sheets. The laths weren't as challenging to move. We put a trashcan at the foot of the stairs and tossed the thin pieces of wood over the railing.

After only three hours, I felt like I was done for the day, having exhausted all my energy and willpower in reserve. I used the locket last night, so I'm extra tired, but I won't be using the locket tonight, most likely not for the next two nights.

If my brother had been blessed with an extra set of arms, he wouldn't have needed me today. My only job now is to hold the sheets of drywall in place while he screws them in.

"You know, they used nail these up."

"Yep, I remember you complaining about that when

you were taking the old sheets down."

After that brief exchange, Gerald turned the radio on. We got the two interior walls done with no problem, but he said he had to put insulation up in the two exterior walls. I offered to help, but he said he only had one "Tyvek suit," whatever that is.

We both went downstairs, and Gerald did something that surprised me.

"Ay, you ever talk to Cedric after the other day?"

Gerald has never shown any concern for any of my relationships.

"I talked to him last night."

"That's good. Seems like a cool guy. I dunno what the problem was. I figured you weren't up to normal yet aftah the hospital."

"It wasn't anything serious."

"Good to hear. In a week or two, soon as everything's wrapped up, I gotta go home. I'll feel better I'm not leaving you here alone."

Chapter 29

Forest Trail

My reputation for ordering the same thing every time has caught up with me, so now I no longer need to order. Soon after I sat in the booth, I was greeted by Tiff's smile. I can't tell if her good mood is forced or natural, but it's definitely contagious. She serves me black coffee and an "I'll get Gus to start your food," before she walks to her next booth. This is a busy morning for her. Four heads at the bar and three tables.

Of course, my company is fashionably late. He's not wearing a brightly colored suit, though. I never thought I would see him in a navy blue suit and white shirt. He waltzes into the diner, nods at the burly guy who turned around as the door opened, and then makes his way over to sit across from me.

"Hey," I greet Cedric as he sits down.

"Good morning, Ms. Emma."

One of the customers at the bar snickers. Cedric furrows his brow toward the man. It's the first time I've seen him the least bit angry.

"We've much to discuss. Perhaps we should go

somewhere with less… distractions," Cedric suggests.

I grab my phone and stand up from the booth.

"Where are the two of you heading off to?" Tiff calls from behind the bar.

"We're just going for a walk," I say. "We'll be back soon."

"Well, don't be too long. Your food'll get cold."

Egressing Danny's Diner, I head toward my car. Cedric stops me and tells me there's a "forest trail" behind the diner. I follow him around to the back of the building. There's a small dumpster, a large black box next to it, and some upside-down trash cans with water flowing from underneath them. The smell isn't great.

A line of dirt cuts across the ten feet of grass between the back of the diner and the forest. Before stepping off the pavement, I look down at my shoes' clean, black leather. My weight shifts to my toes, but there's an invisible wall in front of me. Cedric is already at the end of the section of the trail visible to me. He was about to disappear into the gap in the underbrush before he realized I was not behind him.

"Miss Emma, your shoes will come clean after. If not, there are more shoes in the world."

I sigh. "You're right."

I step onto the dirt trail. It hasn't rained lately, so the loose dirt pushes away from the soles and heels of my shoes. I'm not used to walking through the wilds. Cedric waits for me while I close the gap, and he outstretches his arm in an L shape. I hook my arm around his, and we walk into the forest. For a smoker, he smells more like leather and cinnamon than cigarettes.

The underbrush was only thick around the boundary of the forest. On the interior, it's sparse. Moss and pine nettle blanket most of the land the trees left behind. Ferns and other small bushes with white, yellow, and purple flowers dot the landscape. Were I an illustrator, I would use this as a backdrop for a wolf stalking a girl in a red cloak.

"I have been researching the locket," Cedric says, breaking the silence of our enchanting endeavor. "The Theosian Order has a lot of information, but there is much we don't know about the locket."

"What don't you know about the locket? A lot of the antecessor memories I view have something to do with the locket."

"For starters, we don't know how it went from Amelia Evans's possession to the Oak Cove House."

"I don't know that either. One of the memories I relived was of Amelia, soon after she was commissioned to paint the locket."

"Oh," He says. I wait for him to follow up with something, but he doesn't.

"What's wrong?" I ask.

"I didn't know you used to be Amelia Evans."

"Is that a bad thing?"

"No, I just… I see the resemblance now."

We step up a small but steep hill. I can hear water as soon as we're over the hill. The clouds break, and sunlight beams through the canopy.

"So," I start the conversation again, "What else don't you know about the locket?"

"Well, we know the locket itself was crafted in early Renaissance Era France by a silversmith who was quite prolific, and that is only speculation, as the locket shares the same style as many of his pieces. We have a pretty good idea of where it went after it was a locket, but we have no idea where the material inside the locket came from before that."

"I've seen bits and pieces from its earlier stages. Before it was a locket, it was a sword pommelstone. One of my ancestors, a Viking, stole the sword from a Frisian war chief, but I don't know how it became a pommel stone. Before that, it was an amulet worn by an Egyptian artisan named Aya."

"The Viking Age and Ancient Egypt were thousands of years apart," Cedric says.

"Before Egypt, it was in a Sumerian City, Eridu. It was much larger, though, a mirror in a temple to Ishtar."

Cedric's arm twitches a little. "So, the locket was present in mankind's earliest civilizations?"

"Even earlier. I can't find anything definitive, but the priestess knew the mirror was older than she could comprehend, traded from a far-off land."

"Your antecessors, it seems most of them encountered the locket?"

"The majority of them, yes. I'm trying to figure out if my current life is in the nine out of ten who move the locket along or the one out of ten that live their own life," I say.

"I have a feeling this locket won't be the most significant thing in your life."

I lean against Cedric as we look over the water, but he pulls away. He takes a pack of cigarettes out of his jacket and lights one. He offered to walk me back to the diner and said he had a meeting he needed to get to. I don't press him for any questions. I know I overstepped, and he's trying to add distance between us.

Chapter 30

Meiying

The heady scent of incense fills the air as I stand amidst the opulent splendor of a grand palace, transported to the illustrious Era of the Three Kingdoms in ancient China. The guards at the gate called me Meiying when they welcomed me home. I'm a diplomat representing a king who rules over a realm as vast as his ambitions. The weight of my intricate robes is a constant reminder of the responsibility resting on my shoulders, the duty to navigate the world on behalf of my king and his political interests.

The bustling court is a symphony of colors and movements centered around me as I recount my most recent journey to Emperor Jianhua. His scrutinizing gaze remains fixed on me, a testament to his interest in my words. My mission took me to distant lands, and I describe the fascinating cultures I encountered, the foreign dignitaries with whom I interacted, and the lessons I learned from each encounter.

The memory of a particular encounter lingers most vividly, one with a Roman aristocrat, Custodius Verus, he called himself. He possessed an artifact of undeniable intrigue, a piece of blue metal, ordinary in appearance yet extraordinary in aura. When this piece of jewelry is gazed into under the moonlight, one can see who they were before this life. Last I lived, I was a farmer. I am privileged and honored to serve a king in this life.

Emperor Jianhua's expression softens, his eyes twinkling as I speak of the artifact's allure, the sense of mystery that enveloped it, and the stories it could potentially unlock. I recount the aristocrat's belief that the locket was a vessel through which the threads of time and existence converged, allowing glimpses into lives long faded from memory. Custodius Verus thought the pendant a gift more valuable than anything he had been given.

I reveal my negotiations, the delicate dance of diplomacy, and the aristocrat's reluctance to part with a treasure so potent. As my account reaches its conclusion, I sense the court's anticipation. The king raises a hand to silence one of his other dignitaries as they ask if I acquired the locket. I lament. I was not able to secure this otherworldly prize.

The king's face was motionless for the duration of his pause after my tale ended. My heart raced, and my brow began to sweat as I wondered the nature of the thoughts I assumed to be swirling within his skull. In the pit of my soul, I feel he is disappointed in me for not bringing him a gift so valuable.

When Emperor Jianhua speaks, it is with reassurance. "It is for the better you did not bring me this amulet." Among the court, a varied chorus of breaths plays out. Disappointed exhales clash with the relieved sighs over the king forgiving me. Chatter rests in the corner of the room until the king raises his hand to quiet them once again. "What good is it to view the past, to see someone you no longer are and have no power to affect the circumstances?"

My vision warps and I'm in the Memory Room again

when it clears. The more I use this locket and see my past lives, the more distant I feel from my previous incarnations. Amelia Evans was a successful artist. She had the confidence and creativity necessary to succeed in that field. Astrid's loss seemed to empower her, whereas my losses cripple me. Ishtar looked out for her community, while I've only ever looked after myself. I'm almost thirty. I feel like I've missed my potential. I've done so much more in different lifetimes.

Parts of you persist. Stubbornness, resilience, traits unchanged.

I sigh, "But I struggle with so much the others seemed unburdened by."

Yet, the core remains. Resolve to face challenges, unyielding.

"Meiying was graceful, composed. I'm..." I pause, not sure how to describe myself. "...well, I'm not like that."

Beneath the surface, shared strength. Your core echoes through the ages. Different arenas, same determination. You can't escape yourself.

I still fail to see any resemblance between me and the diplomat. "She played politics. I stumble through life."

The essence, the tenacity, consistent.

"I never faced the complexities she did."

Life shapes differently, but the spirit resonates. The strength within. Lightbulbs—the filament is the same, but the shape, thickness, and color of the globe can all change the outward manifestation.

I think I'm beginning to understand the Guardian's point. "You're saying, despite the differences, there's something of me in all of them?"

Precisely. Strength, determination — timeless. A thread unbroken.

"Maybe... maybe you're right. I need to focus less on the differences."

Acceptance brings clarity. The strength unites,

transcending time.

"Okay. I'll try to see it that way."

Chapter 31

Open

"Hey, Emmy," Gerald says as I load the coffee maker. "You should probably make yahself scarce today. I'm gonna be all ovah the place, doing some finishing wahk, making shoah this place is nice and good for you."

"That's good with me. I can take my laptop down to Danny's, get my work done for today, and come back this afternoon."

"Yeah, that's for the best. I'm gonna be swinging hammers and stuff."

"It's good," I tell him. I don't care what he does as long as my house is fixed. I almost miss the dereliction as opposed to the construction site. The smells of exposed timber, plaster, and insulation are getting to me.

I catch myself getting excited about being outside of my house. I get to leave my cave. Anyone can find me. I could meet anyone in the world today. I'll be open to anything. Moving to this foreign town and finding the locket, I think, is changing me. A couple months ago, the thought of seeing an overly enthusiastic waitress at a diner where if one person is having a conversation, everyone is having a conversation, would have scared me to death. In fact, I could barely talk to Tiff the first time I met her.

***

Of course, Tiff isn't at Danny's today. The new waitress seems more… muted. She's slight, petite, with straight, dark hair. It's the uncanny valley. Seeing someone other than Tiff waiting tables at the diner gives a pang of dread. Instead of letting that dread overcome me and trigger my anxiety, I push it down. I wanted to be open today, I remind myself.

"Good morning," the waitress beams, suddenly donning the attitude of Tiff. "I'm Cindy. I'll be your waitress today. Say, I haven't seen you here before."

I unzip my laptop carry bag. "I'm Emma. I come in here pretty often. I just moved here about a month ago. Usually, Tiff is waiting on me."

"Oh yeah!" Cindy's smile defies my expectations of reality and widens. It takes a special breed of person to wait tables, I suppose. "Tiff told me about you. You're the one who bought the Oak Cove House."

"That's me," I answer.

Cindy returns, puts a mug in front of me, and fills it with coffee from what looks like a freshly brewed pot. "Cream or sugar?" she asks.

"No, not for me."

"So, what kind of work do you do?" Cindy asks, pointing to my laptop, now waiting for my password.

"Accounting."

"Oh, I was never good with numbers."

"Accounting is actually a lot simpler than people think. It's mostly just addition, subtraction, multiplication, division, and percents."

"I only know my times tables up to ten," Cindy says.

"I don't even know what a times table is, and I make six figures a year doing this."

"Well, I just had a baby a couple months ago. My dad

owns this diner, and my husband's an electrician. I think I have a good thing going as is. Can I get you something for breakfast?"

"Yes. Two slices of turkey bacon, crispy, one egg, over easy, and some home fries."

"Sounds like a good breakfast. I'll get my brother started on it."

"Thanks." I always suspected this was a family business, but I would never have guessed Tiff wasn't in the family. Maybe she is, but Cindy fits this puzzle better than Tiff.

Now that my laptop is up and running, I plug in the USB stick to let me use cell phone data. Emails– nothing out of the ordinary. Interim reports are due soon, but everything looks good. I check over the spreadsheets. There's nothing to reconcile between our expenses and revenue reports, so my work is done in two hours, three cups of coffee, and seven hundred calories.

Cindy had left me alone for the most part, but once she saw I had closed my laptop, she got chatty again.

"Another day at the office in the books?"

"It seems that way."

"Say, do you have any dinner plans? Now that I'm back in the game, we can do weekend dinner shifts again. Richie has a couple of prime ribs he's about to throw in for tonight, and we'll have some of our usual lunch stuff available, too."

"Well, I'm three minutes away, and my brother's visiting. Gerald loves prime rib, so I'm sure I can convince him to come in."

"Wonderful!"

Ethan McGrane

Chapter 32

My Hometown

Gerald was almost drooling when he parked his pickup truck in front of Danny's. "It's been years since I've had a good king cut."

Immediately inside the diner, a girl, probably still in junior high, greets us behind a lectern taken right out of a church. The large cross carved into the front of it makes me positive the shelves inside have prayer booklets.

After a quick smile, the hostess tells us to "take a menu and sit where there's room."

I haven't seen Danny's this packed before. I wasn't sure Gerald and I would find a seat, but as luck would have it, our formally yet vibrantly dressed friend was in the corner booth and waved the two of us over to sit with him. The orange dusklight pouring through the window splashes across Cedric's dark green suit, with a cream-colored shirt.

I didn't recognize the man sitting across the booth from Cedric by the back of his white hair-covered head. But when he turned to greet me and Gerald, I remembered him.

"Mr. Henry, You've met Miss Emma, yes?"

"Ah, yes. The young lady who bought the Oak Cove

House." Henry gestures toward Gerald, "Is this your husband?"

"My brother, Gerald," I say as I sit beside Cedric. "He's helping me fix the house up."

"Wonderful," Henry says.

Tiff swings by our table. After we order our drinks—cokes all the way around, Tiff smiles in reply to Henry's remark about how packed the diner is.

"Oh, we got this handled. I've got my kids here tonight. They're still working off their summer camps."

Being one of the few people I've engaged with regularly since moving to South Thornbrook, I feel like I should have known Tiff had children. Her seemingly one-track mind and unbreakable character as a "cheery waitress" led me to believe she was alone outside her job.

Cedric pulls me back to reality from my wandering thoughts. "Mr. Henry has something for you, Miss Emma."

I look across the table as Henry clears his throat. "Ah, yes. After our last discussion, it bothered me that I didn't know anything about the previous owner of the Oak Cove House, so I did some digging. Unfortunately, I couldn't find much, but I did get a name, Arnold Hastings."

I glance over at Cedric, who shifts slightly in the seat, and then I turn back to Henry. "I appreciate you looking. It's more information than I had before."

After that exchange, it was all small talk for the rest of our evening together. Gerald stole the show toward the end. Henry was absolutely enamored with Gerald's stories of weird things he'd seen in people's houses as a contractor. My mind was distracted, though. I need to find Arnold Hastings. As the previous owner, he can fill in the last blanks about the locket and the Guardian.

Chapter 33

Lyra

Looking down at the city of Athens from the Acropolis is a sight available to those in modernity, but looking at ancient Athens from this vantage is a sight afforded only to me now. I am Lyra, a fledgling philosopher in a world of thinkers and intellectuals. My mind is a fortress of skepticism, fortified by rationality, materialism, and shunning anything beyond the tangible. The notion of supernatural beings, reincarnation, and an immortal soul is folly to me, for I have no proof of such things.

Amidst the courtyard of our academy, I encounter Zenon—a respected philosopher whose views starkly contrast mine. Zenon speaks of an artifact he calls the Memory Shard, a vessel to the past lives of the user. His words weave a narrative of souls interconnected through time.

Intrigued, I listen as Zenon reveals the amulet—an unassuming object brimming with the potential to unravel the mysteries of existence. As he offers it to me, I hesitate. My rational mind resists it, dismissing it as mere superstition. But curiosity gets the better of me.

Gazing into the reflective, blue-gray metal, my reality fragments. I am transported to a memory—a past life. I stand as a warrior on a battlefield, feeling the weight of a sword in my hand and the echo of a battle cry. The sensations are vivid and undeniable, and I'm shaken.

Stunned, I return to the moonlit courtyard, my penchant for denying the supernatural, my facade of physicality crumbling like days-old bread. Zenon watches with knowing eyes, his expression blending understanding and compassion. He extends an invitation to explore further, to journey into my past lives, and challenge the confines of my beliefs. He didn't show me the shard to destroy my creeds, but to correct them.

Resisting doubt, I succumb to curiosity and embrace the Memory Shard again. This time, I'm transported to a quiet village, where I tend to crops and share laughter with a family that isn't mine in this lifetime. Each memory shatters another piece of my skepticism, revealing glimpses of lives I never imagined.

I debate with Zenon and our fellow philosophers, sharing my newfound experiences. My words are met with skepticism and curiosity from my peers. I question the nature of reality, the existence of the soul, and the interconnectedness of all lives. The others have seen my change of heart and wonder if Zenon will ever grant them use of the Memory Shard.

During a moment of introspection in the courtyard beneath the Acropolis, I feel a profound connection—a whisper from the past, transcending the present. It's as if the spirits of ancient thinkers are guiding me through the corridors of time, urging me to embrace the mysteries waiting beyond the rational realm.

This vision does something I've not experienced before. When I was Astrid, it skipped forward in her life several times, but this one seems to play at high speed. Lyra's journey unfolds. Her skepticism wanes, replaced by wonder and awe. Given to her was a revelation to forever alter her understanding of existence. The Memory Shard showed her soul traverse lifetimes, leaving echoes resonating across millennia. I feel months of Lyra's life pass faster than eyes can blink. I feel her become happier once she comes to terms with the larger picture of human existence, how we are creatures both sacred and profane.

The moment arrives when my journey as Lyra concludes, and I return to my own life. My mind remains within the philosophical realm of ancient Athens. The shattered fragments of skepticism realign with what I know as Em– myself. I close my eyes, picturing the view of the city from the acropolis. As I gaze upon Athens, I take solace in the fact that the past is never truly lost, and the locket lets me view the resounding echoes within my soul.

We should find virtue in seeking the truth, whether or not it aligns with our current notions.

Noble. But I feel no closer to the answers I want.

"I'm going to do all I can to help you."

No answer.

Ethan McGrane

Chapter 34

Small Steps

Cedric asked me to meet him at Rusty's this afternoon. When I got there, he had one empty bottle of cheap beer in front of him, and then he bought the top-shelf bottle of scotch, and the two of us got into his car. He drove us north, a little past the outskirts of South Thornbrook.

Without much warning, he stopped on a gravel patch on the side of the road and got out of the car. He hadn't told me where we were going, and I didn't think this was the place. He tapped on the window and ushered me out onto the gravel.

We walked on a wide trail. The two of us could walk comfortably side by side, and a passersby would have enough space to go around us. I wanted to hold Cedric's hand, but his left hand was clutched around the bottle of scotch, so I hooked my right thumb into my pocket and bade my time.

The forest gave way to stones, the stones gave way to gravel, and the gravel gave way to smooth, light-colored sand. Cedric escorted me to a couple of rocks resting in the sand. They were dry, perfectly shaped to sit on and watch the sky darken in the east while the sun illuminated the sky above us in orange.

I'm familiar with the concept of watching a sunset, but what are we watching facing east? I've never heard of watching a "night rise." So, I ask Cedric what we're doing here.

"I'm going to make you feel better," he answers, tearing the foil off the top of the bottle of scotch. "You see, I think one of the reasons you're so anxious about the locket, about discovering its history, is because you've never experienced magic before," He pulls the cork free of the bottle with a cartoonish pop and takes a sip. "When you step into the world of magic, it is the same world as the one you've always lived in, but now the world doesn't play by the same rules. It's best to take small steps." He passes the bottle to me.

I take a sip. It burns, and I almost don't have the strength to keep it down. "So…" speaking causes the alcohol in my breath to burn my airways, "…what is the baby step you're going to show me?"

"Drink more. A sober mind will ignore it."

I take another sip. It's easier than the first but still quite harsh. Notes of caramel and smoke tickle my palette on the tail end.

"There is much magic in the world. I don't want your experience with the locket and the Guardian to sour your taste for it." He motions for me to drink more, and I oblige. Part of the third sip comes back up, and I pass the bottle back to Cedric.

A bird calls in the distance. Cedric remarks on how eagles typically make that noise in the morning. Maybe one day I'll get to know Cedric's more non-occult interests. But his previous point in the conversation brought up something I thought about after my memory as Lyra last night.

"This isn't the first time my soul has encountered the locket, but it's the first time I've encountered a guardian for the locket. My antecessors, even Amelia Evans, my most recent antecessor, the only obstacle for them to use the locket, amulet, sword pommel stone, or mirror, was daylight. As far as I can tell, there was never a guardian spirit before.”

“That's one of the things that worries me,” Cedric says. “Even Master Crosby, the founder of the Theosian Order, who studied the locket extensively before he sent it to America, never wrote anything about the locket having a guardian.”

“So, whoever had the locket between the time it disappeared with Amelia Evans–” I hiccup. “...and the time I discovered it in the Oak Cove House has to be responsible for the Guardian.”

“We need to find Mr. Arnold Hastings,” Cedric concludes.

We sat there on the rocks, drinking the scotch that would be better served if it were on the rocks like us. I asked Cedric a few times what we were out here for. Each time, he told me to keep drinking. Eventually, I slurred my speech when I asked him the same question, and he told me to keep drinking. The moon became our only light, and I forgot what I wanted to ask him before getting to the end of the question, to which he only pointed out to the water and said, “Look!”

Out on the water, lights were hovering above the choppy surface. There were seven in total. Little orbs of light, swaying back and forth, never getting close enough to touch each other as if they were performing a dance they'd rehearsed several times. The lights began to flicker, and each time the light dimmed, a musical note filled my ears, but only my ears. It wasn't like when the Guardian speaks to me, where I feel his words directly in the center of my skull. The notes were flute-like, and each color orb played a different note.

At first, the music was quite welcoming and peaceful, but eventually, it warped and became dismal and hopeless. It twisted into anger before reaching a happy tune. Parts of it sounded like they were trying to sell men cheap deodorant, but overall, it felt magical. Whether it was the scotch or the ethereal music troupe, I felt complete peace wash over me as the lights faded from reality.

Tears streamed down Cedric's face. Seeing his display of emotion almost overwhelmed me, bringing me into a similar state. But I suppressed the feelings. The performance wasn't sad for me. Maybe Cedric had a different show played for him?

Cedric's plan worked, though. I felt like the locket, and what was happening to me wasn't insurmountable. There's more magic in the world than I knew. I turn to Cedric, "Magic lockets, past lives, demons... I didn't believe in any of that before I bought that house."

"I didn't believe in any of that either... until my brother died."

Chapter 35

A Light in the Attic

Around three in the morning, Cedric had sobered up enough to drive me home. I tried to coax him into explaining what happened to his brother, but he would say some variation of "I was drunk. I shouldn't have let that slip."

I was in a stupor all the way from exiting Cedric's car to entering my house, fumbling for the light switch to turn on the hanging lamp in the foyer and struggling up the stairs. Gerald sanded the stairs to the point where they now look like raw lumber, even though the wood is probably older than I am. The steps are so smooth I lost traction several times. He did a little bit past the steps, too, but not much. I turn the corner to the upstairs hallway, and my stomach sinks as I see the attic stairs are down.

My heart races as I climb the stairs, and I'm out of breath when I reach the top. Halfway through my climb, I lost my balance and thought I would fall. But I made it. The overhead light was on in the attic, just a light socket dangling from the ceiling, with a pull cord hanging from it. It was an empty socket when I was Lyra. Having a bulb now may mean Gerald is sleeping in the living room and forgot to turn off the light when he went downstairs, or it could mean my fear is warranted.

I force myself forward to the Memory Room. I haven't been this scared to enter the sanctum since I first discovered it.

My fears were confirmed as I entered the Memory Room. Gerald was standing, half stooped over the side table, frozen in place, staring into the open locket he held in his left hand.

I stepped forward, intending to shake him out of the trance, but my body froze, and *STOP* flooded my mind.

The damage is already done… don't pull him out of his memory.

I can't fight the Guardian, so I retreat. I returned to the second floor and sat on the top step. I'll wait for Gerald to come downstairs on his own. I'm sure there will be a lot he wants to talk about.

***

I had a splitting headache just before sunrise when Gerald shook me awake. His eyes were bloodshot, and he seemed out of it. When he sits down next to me on the top step, I'm unsure how to start the conversation about how he spent his night. I don't know how he feels about it. His using the locket revealed I've been lying to him since he got here.

"So that's what you been doing in the attic? You got a locket that shows you history like you was there?"

I clear my throat before starting. "It lets you relive memories from your past lives."

Gerald takes a long pause. The Guardian must not have spoken to him. I think my first assumption was correct. He just went up there to change the lightbulb and then got curious. But what is Gerald going through right now? Maybe I shouldn't have told him what he saw was one of his antecessors.

"I was in medieval Europe, I think. People were

talking in a way I didn't undahstan, but deep down, I didn't have to. I even spoke it a couple times. I was building a house for my nephew and his newly-wed wife." Gerald yawns halfway through the word wife, reminding me of what the locket costs in the present.

"You can't use the locket too often," I say.

"I don't evah want to use it again."

I was surprised by his response.

"Look, you got some spooky shit happening in this house. I'm going to finish fixing this place up. I pretty much only gotta paint and do some small things here and there. I'm leaving as soon as I can."

"I understand."

Chapter 36

Lydia Bianchi

The locket hangs from my fingers. I close my eyes. When I reopen my eyes, the locket still hangs before me, but I and my surroundings have changed. As I gaze into its intricate patterns, I become a young alchemist apprentice in the bustling streets of Renaissance Venice. I am Lydia, a woman whose thirst for knowledge rivaled the currents of the Grand Canal, gaining the attention of a master alchemist.

In the workshop of my mentor, Antonio Rossi, vials of multicolored liquids line the shelves, and the air hums with the promise of secrets yet unveiled. The locket rests before me, a riddle that defies the wisdom of sages. I aim to decipher the material from which it's crafted, a puzzle that consumes my thoughts like the alchemical fires that burn beneath our crucibles.

Antonio, a man with wisdom etched upon his face, examines the locket with curiosity. "Lydia, this is no ordinary object. Its origins are as elusive as the mercury with which we seek to heal various afflictions."

I nod, my determination unwavering. "I shall uncover its essence. Whether it be an amalgam of elements or a substance from realms beyond our understanding, I shall fathom it."

Days blur into nights as I labor in the workshop, performing experiments that test the limits of my alchemical acumen. I subject the locket to fires that rival the forge of Hephaestus himself, yet its surface remains unblemished, a testament to its enigmatic constitution.

In the labyrinthine streets of Venice, I seek knowledge from fellow alchemists, weaving my way through arcane conversations and whispered rumors. A cryptic figure whispers of the legendary "Aetherium," a substance rumored to bridge the gap between the earthly and ethereal planes. Could this be the material from which the locket was wrought?

As the sun dips below the horizon, casting shadows upon the canals, I return to Antonio's workshop with a heart brimming with hope. I present the possibility of Aetherium to my master, whose eyes widen with both admiration and caution. "Aetherium is a myth, a fable spun by alchemists for generations. To seek it is to tread upon the precipice of futility."

Undeterred, I resolve to journey deeper into the enigma. The locket's surface, illuminated by the sunlight, glimmers with the promise of secrets from eons past. It is as if the locket itself yearns to reveal its origin, whispering secrets in the language of ancient souls.

I performed a final experiment in a secluded alcove by the Venetian waterfront. Drawing upon the alchemical arts, I channel the elements and conjure a resonance that transcends the material realm. The locket responds, emitting a gentle hum that resonates with the frequencies of distant stars.

A vision washes over me—an image of a realm bathed in ethereal light, where souls intertwine like threads in a cosmic tapestry. It is a glimpse into the Aetherium, the elusive substance that defies the boundaries of earth and sky.

I return to Antonio's Laboratory, the weight of newfound knowledge etched upon my features. "Master Antonio, the locket is forged from Aetherium. It binds both the mundane and the mystic."

Antonio's eyes sparkle with a mix of pride and awe. "Lydia, you've done it." With a rush of excitement, I'm wrapped in Antonio's embrace. But, at that moment, the memory warps. I'm still Lydia, and I'm still in Venice, but the laboratory sits vacant, half burned. Its owner has long since gone. He owed money to dangerous people. They took anything valuable and burned the rest. Antonio didn't have the heart to recover, and without a master, I was just a fledgling alchemist nobody would give the time of day to.

In the Memory Room, the Guardian seems irritated. *The locket must be aligning with your intentions. You care more for your selfish pursuit of knowledge than freeing me.*

I don't answer. Once I leave the Memory Room, my thoughts are safe from the Guardian's peering presence. I know the Guardian can be dangerous. I need a contingency. I need Cedric.

Ethan McGrane

Chapter 37

Goodbye

"You gonna see me out?" Gerald asks.

"Would I hear the end of it if I didn't?"

"Probably not. When you coming down to visit?"

I pause. I promised Gerald I would go down to Groton for Liam's upcoming birthday, but if I don't have the locket figured out… well, the spirit living in the attic, I can't go more than a couple miles outside town.

"You don't have to answer that now," Gerald says. He must have seen the gears turning in my head. I hope he doesn't think I've returned to my old ways. I'm not the antisocial shut-in I was a month ago. I look toward the ground behind him, avoiding eye contact with him.

Gerald's expression softens. "Hey, just be careful. You've got weird spooky shit going on in this house. I'm half thinking about staying here and calling a priest to help you sort this out."

"Cedric is helping me."

"Well, then I'm going to assume you're in good hands with that. But don't cut me off. Liam's at the age now where he will notice if you're not there, and kids don't forget that stuff. I'm still paying dividends on some of my mistakes with Emily, Olivia, and Sophia."

"Girls can be cruel."

Gerald's expression hardens again, with his brows furrowing. "It would be a big step in the right direction for you. The kids hardly know you, and after that trip to the hospital, even Gina's asking about how you're doing. I know you'd be happier if you were involved in their lives. So, you come down for Liam's birthday, you have a good time, and then we'll come up here for Thanksgiving. I'm not going to beg you anymore. You want to act like you've made progress. This is your chance to prove it."

I meet Gerald's eyes and make sure to maintain contact as I say, "I promise I won't miss Liam's birthday."

Gerald wraps his arms around me. His bear hug isn't as overbearing as it was the first time it occurred on my front porch. It feels more natural, like my brother is embracing me instead of a stranger trying to comfort me. Tears well in my eyes, and I have to keep myself from blinking so they don't stream through my makeup.

When Gerald finally lets go, he looks at me. He can see the tears. I know he can see them. His voice, low, raspy, half-broken, says, "Goodbye, Emmy."

Gerald walks toward his truck. He opens the door, swings his backpack to the passenger seat, and before he climbs in, in a tone almost hysteric, somewhere I can't chart between laughing and crying, he shouts, "I'll see you in a couple weeks!"

I let the tears fall as soon as Gerald disappears over the hill. I walk into the house he helped me fix. The smooth, recently lacquered wood floor barely makes a noise as I step across it to get to the armchair in the living room. I sink into it and mull over the TV remote. I finally have my home, but I'm alone in it for the first time. I have no neighbors. I could disappear like Arnold Hastings did, and nobody would notice for days.

Chapter 38

Breakthrough

I wasn't alone the next day, though. Cedric said he found something important and wanted to show me in person. I'm not used to playing host, but the house is already immaculate since the renovations recently ended.

I watched from the living room window as Cedric parked his car and got out. He's wearing the same periwinkle linen suit he had on the first time I saw him. But he's got a plain white undershirt and no tie. It looks like he's just arrived from giving a sermon. I know better, though.

From the backseat, Cedric grabs a leatherbound book and then, without haste, crosses the stretch of gravel between his car and my house. I open the door for him before he reaches the porch. While exchanging greetings, I ushered him into the living room. Before I can sit on the couch, though, Cedric says this matter is more appropriate to discuss in my office.

So, I sat at my desk, in front of my closed laptop, and Cedric sat in one of the chairs I kept on the other side of the desk to inflate my ego. At first, he looked as though he was going to toss the notebook onto my desk, but he hesitated momentarily before gently laying it on the solid oak surface.

"I had a breakthrough in my research."

I look at him blankly. "Go on."

"Arnold Hastings. He was the previous owner of the Oak Cove House."

We already knew that, but I couldn't tell if he paused for emphasis or a response.

"He never sold this house. The county seized it ten years after he disappeared. He was a partner at a prestigious law firm in DC but vanished off the earth while vacationing here in the summer of 2006."

"So, he owns the house, disappears, and then I buy the house about two decades later."

"Well, it's deeper than that." Cedric flips the notebook open to where he had the bookmark. "I think Arnold Hastings is the Guardian." He points to a paragraph in his notebook. I skim through it for a second.

"Disembodied spirits, those who cannot remember who they were during their lifetime but are certain they were at one point human, are often those who died by untimely, unnatural means. For example, if someone were to cast a spell, a binding, a ward, or even use a magical artifact that requires more energy than the subject has access to, it can result in the immolation of the body and a soul trapped in the essence of the host body's surroundings. Since the separation of body and soul is instant, the memories stored in the physical body, such as brain matter, will not transfer to the soul. These spirits often have extreme control in an exceedingly localized area."

My jaw had dropped by the end of the passage. "Where did you find this?"

"One of my colleagues from the Theosian Order is conducting research at the Bennington Triangle in Vermont. I drove out to visit him the day after we watched the fae dance at the beach. He specializes in spirits, whereas I specialize in artifacts."

My brows press together involuntarily. "So, if I tell the Guardian he is Arnold Hastings, will he 'move on' to the afterlife and leave me alone?"

Cedric's eyes widen. "No! Under no circumstance do you tell him. It's not like the ghost movies where you help a spirit find closure, and then they move on to peace and happiness. If you tell the Guardian their true identity, they will likely become angered that they still can't remember, and when spirits are angered, they are unpredictable. The Guardian could crush your heart in an instant if you anger him."

"What do I do, then?"

"Keep using the locket at your normal pace. Appease the Guardian. You say he wants you to find out why the locket is here. Do what he says in the meantime, and I will find a way to get rid of him."

The thought of helping a spirit who can kill me on a whim doesn't ease any of my worries. It amplifies my anxieties. With a shaking hand, I point to the notebook. "I-Is there anything in there that could help us?"

"Maybe, but I'm going to have to dig through it. Thad is out of cellphone signal, so I'd have to drive back out there if I need to talk with him again."

"What if I just stop visiting the Memory Room altogether until you figure out how to get rid of the Guardian?"

"You told me before that he can make your life uncomfortable here, and you have nowhere else to go. You can't leave town."

"Well, I guess I have no choice but to trust you to sort the Guardian out."

"I won't let you down, Miss Emma."

Chapter 39

Eleanor Harrison

I set foot in the Memory Room for the first time since learning my ethereal host's identity. Upon opening the same locket that claimed Arnold Hastings's life, I am no longer Emma. I stand amidst the dimly lit parlor of the Shadewood Boarding House in a part of England bearing the same name as the previous owner of my house. Hastings, England, a setting from the annals of history. I am in the company of two enigmatic occultists—Aldric Crosby and his secretary, Kieran Graham. Aldric founded the Theosian Order, which seems to be my only ally in handling this nightmare I've fled into.

Aldric's aura is striking. His piercing gaze holds an unfathomable universe of secrets. Seated across from him, Kieran Graham exudes an air of loyalty and dedication transcending the boundaries of a mere working relationship. In Kieran's eyes, I see the same gaze toward Aldric that my son looks at his father with.

The parlor resonates with the timbre of their conversation, a discussion that dances on the edge of the arcane. The locket rests on a small table between them, its presence weighing down the room. It gleams with an otherworldly luster. I feel inconsequential in this memory, as though Eleanor Harrison is present in this meeting but not active.

Crosby's fingers trace patterns in the incense smoke. His passive demeanor is contrasted by his voice, laced with urgency. "Kieran, we must ensure the locket reaches its destination safely. America holds the promise of protection—a sanctuary where its secrets will remain guarded."

Kieran nods, his expression a blend of reverence and resolve. "The locket carries echoes of past lives, a tapestry of souls intertwined through time. It is a bounty of mysteries we must not allow to fall into the wrong hands."

Aldric Crosby sips his tea and exhales deeply. Though invisible, the air expelled from his nostrils swirls like incense in the room's atmosphere. "The Nazis know of the locket. When they took France, where this very locket was smithed, they gained confirmation of what they previously only had whispers and innuendo. There's no telling how this war will end. If only the ministry accepted my help, the fighting could have ended years ago."

Crosby's eyes, microcosms of mysticism, meet mine as though he gazes through time itself. It's as if he senses my presence—my role as an observer from another era. A smile curls upon his lips, a knowing affirmation that the threads of destiny are woven across ages. He glances at Kieran, "The matter we discussed earlier, our good friend, Miss Green…"

Kieran looks confused and redirects Aldric to the matter at hand.

"We entrust the lockets journey not to the winds of fate," Crosby declares, his voice a melody resonating with the ebb and flow of cosmic tides. "Across the Atlantic, to a land where its mysteries shall remain veiled from those who seek to exploit its power. Take it home with you. But, do take care to not give into its power. Overuse can have… undesirable side effects."

Kieran's hand hovers over the locket, a guardian's touch bridging past and present. "May the spirits of old and the guardians of time watch over its voyage, ensuring its safe passage to distant shores."

The parlor pulsates with a potent energy. My heart quickens, for I am a mere observer of this reverberation through the corridors of history. A reverberation spiraling my fragile life out of control in the present.

Crosby's words ring with finality, sealing the locket's fate in the annals of destiny. "To America, it shall go, a gift to the land of dreams. There, it shall rest until the hour of revelation beckons."

With a nod, Kieran gently picks up the locket and offers it to me. The moment is frozen in time—a convergence of an ancient narrative's minds, souls, and threads. Aldric stares at me, his face postured inquisitively, but his eyes and mouth, a piercing smile boring into my soul.

As I return to the present, the echoes of that fateful discussion linger.

That was a step in the right direction. Ancient history won't help me much.

Ethan McGrane

Chapter 40

Terminated

"We need you to come back to the office." Veronica, the Human Resources Specialist from Tally Venture Financing, tells me.

"I'm a bit tied up at the moment. How soon do you need me?"

"ASAP. The CFO spotted some pretty large discrepancies in last month's report."

I covered the microphone for a moment and sighed. I should have been paying more attention. I've been too busy dealing with everything here, though.

"I need a date, a time, something I can plan on. I moved to a different state, and I'm still fixing up the house I bought."

"There's a department meeting on Thursday. If you aren't planning on being there, I suggest you take a few minutes to email me your resignation. This discrepancy might get us investigated, and since you're a senior accountant, there might be some blame on you."

"Ok," I try to steady my voice. "I'll let you know by the end of today."

Without any farewells, the call goes dead. Our HR department has always been a nightmare. One time, they made Mandy cry. I don't know the details for that, though. Mandy wouldn't talk about it.

I need to resign. I'm the only person they could blame for the mess. I've been working remotely and haven't been paying attention to my work as I should have been. What would I say to them, anyway? "Sorry, things have been hectic. I've been dealing with ghosts and a locket older than human civilization."

I should be able to coast for a while. The renovations have only taken a third of my savings. Accounting is a valuable skill, so if I need to, I can get a new job in under a week. With the internet being how it is, I don't even have to leave my house to get hired.

Once my laptop boots, I make my way to my company email. I scroll down my contacts. Where is she? She has a weird last name. I wish these were in alphabetical order. I pause for a few moments over *Amanda Wright*. Do I want to leave the company Mandy and I worked for together? This job is one of the last things I still have that the two of us shared.

I could practically hear Dr. Calloway's voice telling me I needed to embrace my new life here. So, I scroll past Mandy, even though it feels like I'm saying goodbye to her all over again, and I keep scrolling until I find *Veronica Blevins*.

I type out a short, sweet, and perhaps overly formal resignation letter. I read over it several times, used my browser's built-in tools to ensure the tone matched my intention, and then hit send and closed my laptop. I sink back into my chair.

As a silver lining, at least I can focus more on the "spooky shit" I have going on in this house now.

Chapter 41

The Origin

Cedric and I have a new system for when I use the locket. The Guardian can read minds. I know who he was, but he doesn't, and there's no telling how he'll react when he finds out. So, staying true to the system, I text Cedric before I enter the attic, and I'll have six hours to check in with him before he comes to help me. I don't know what form his help will take, nor does he. He says he hit a dead end in his research, and he's going to drive out to see his friend Thaddeus after I'm done this session with the locket.

Every time I step into the Memory Room, I could die. I've decided I would rather die in search of the truth than live without the answers.

Welcome back.

I don't respond, unsure of what to say.

I wonder what the locket will show you tonight?

"Let's find out."

I sit in the chair and snatch the locket from the table. I hold it before me, close my eyes, and take a few deep breaths. My heart is racing, each breath hitches in my lungs. I click the locket open. There's no point in delaying this any further. I open my eyes, and reality warps around me.

What surrounded me when the warping reality calms was unprecedented. Barren rock sits under my… feet? I don't have a physical body in this memory. From what I can see, my shape is still human, with two arms, a body, and two legs. I am a specter of energy. My being is composed of tendrils of pale blue and lavender-hued light, with sprinklings of what look like distant stars coursing within them.

This form bears an uncanny resemblance to paintings rendered by Amelia Evans. All my fascination over my incorporeal form distracted me from the source of the pink-orange hue of the sheen along the edges of the barren black rock of the ground. A nebula dominates the majority of the otherwise dark and vacant sky.

A crowd appears around me. I'm suddenly in the midst of a sea of other souls like me. Without communicating with each other, we form a ring. Another ring appears around us, populated by beings similar to us, but orange and red in color. This outer ring seems odd, their bodies shimmering erratically. In the center of our blue circle, a single soul appears.

This soul in the center is twice the size of anyone else. Their aura emanates an energy, an excitement I've never felt before. Their color is violet. The souls in my ring, I can feel their emotions. There is reverence but also collegiality toward the violet god. In the outer circle, there is fear but a steadfast resolve to hear out the god.

Pure white light flashes across the violet god's body, and images fill my mind. Images of a small blue planet interspersed with lush green continents. I recognize it as Earth but with less desert land. In both rings, all of us begin to emit a collective white glow.

The god has given us a gift. Finally, there is a place in the cosmos, a physical location populated with physical beings capable of sustaining our souls for a lifetime. Us star children are energy borrowed from the universe. We've spent eons awaiting such a place. A place to experience emotion, to indulge in flavors unafforded us. Mortality, the ultimate high, can finally be ours.

But, there's a rule: to inhabit a physical life, this violet god requires we lock our memories away, only to be reaccessed after our physical body has ended its earthly journey. The orange and red souls embarked with haste, and so did many in the blue ring. Most of us in the inner ring grasped the magnitude of what we were about to do and hesitated on whether we wanted to subject ourselves to it. The implications… to hell with the implications, I decide. I gaze upon the violet god again, and the vision ends in a flash of white light.

How pleasant it must be… to see the origin of human spirits.

The cusp of my fathom. I don't believe I was meant to see such things.

Chapter 42

Aletheia

After the profundity of the previous night's endeavor, I couldn't help but use the locket again. When I texted Cedric I was going into the Memory Room, he objected at first, warning me of the side effects of overusing the locket and his being out of range to help me if anything goes wrong. I responded that I can handle this.

"I hope I can handle this," I whisper to myself as I approach the door in the attic.

Two nights in a row? A rare sight.

I walk over to the chair and sit down.

No conversation?

"You're not usually in a talking mood."

True, but you are.

I swipe the locket from the table and dangle it before me as I close my eyes and perform my breathing ritual. I click the locket open. I've already been transported into the memory when I open my eyes. I don't have the locket. I didn't travel through the reality-warping kaleidoscope. It jarred me to the point my vision in the memory shimmered, and I thought I would be uprooted from it and brought back to the Memory Room.

I'm standing on a balcony. A gray brick-paved road runs perpendicular to my perch, at least fifty feet below. The street's opposite side is lined with marble, stone, steel, and timber buildings. The architecture is somewhere between what I've seen in Ancient Athens and Eridu. An ocean stretches to the horizon on the other side of the structures. Wooden ships dot the sea. The vessels are mighty, with flat decks, square sails, and oars emerging from their sides like a cell's cilia.

Someone on the street calls, "Aletheia!" I turn my head towards a stocky man pulling a cart. The cart's payload is concealed from the public eye by a tarp, but my cousin brings me a treasure not of this world.

I draw back the curtain separating the balcony from the bedroom. It's a simple area, little more than a bed with several trunks. Scrolls are piled on top of and around one of the trunks. I'm intrigued to know more about those scrolls. But, to my antecessor, those scrolls are just another mundanity.

A tight staircase spirals down, and the space is barely large enough to accommodate me. The walls of smooth clay brush against my arms on several occasions. Halfway down the staircase, an alcove bears an oil lamp and a vase painted with ancient urbanscapes. The top of the alcove is black from the lamp.

The bottom of the stairs let out into a small hallway, leading to a cavernous room again with sparse furniture. A small table in the middle of some chairs mimics the chest in the bedroom, scrolls piled on top of it in whichever orientation they fell. My cousin, Zetetes, is leaning in the doorway.

"Bring the cart around back to the large door. You've done this before."

The ox of a man spins on the ball of his foot and exits

the door. I turn to my left and pass through a large wooden door that I have to shoulder open because of how heavy it is. The space past this door looks like a cartoon dwarf lives here. The floor is dark gray stone, and the walls are carved out of the same stone. Tools hang on the walls, and workbenches line the room with half-finished mechanisms strewn about them. In the center of the space, a large firepit sits dormant. Gray and black coals sit lifelessly, waiting for the moment they are needed.

The far side of the room has large bronze doors. The dark metal has started to green around the edges. A wooden contraption is mounted at the top of the door frame, and a winch is affixed to the wall, with ropes and cords connecting to the contraption. I crank the winch to the right, and the doors open in small, stuttering motions.

My eyes adjust to the sunlight, and I have the mental equivalent of a gasp. A small ramp descends a couple of feet to a paved path that immediately hooks to the right through a small lawn. The end of the lawn is bordered by a large retaining wall that drops into the water. The retaining wall looks like concrete. Where in history am I?

The canal behind my house is massive, at least three hundred feet across. More triremes navigate the waters in an orderly fashion, their sailors' shanties echoing over each other. A large, circular island sits on the other side of the canal. Mighty walls stretch at least a hundred feet into the air. Towering buildings, and a domineering acropolis are all housed within those walls.

"Did Zetetes get lost?" I mutter under my breath. I take the five steps down the ramp and follow the path around the side of my home. My cousin is stopped in front of the cart, chatting with the neighbor girl.

"Zetetes!"

My cousin looks at me, half scowling, half smiling, and tells the neighbor, "Sorry, looks like I have to go now."

"I have matters to get to as well," the neighbor says.

Zetetes grunts as he hoists the cart handles up to his hips and walks forward. I spot him on the corners to help him navigate to the ramp and climb it. Once the cart is entirely inside the doors, I crank the winch to the left to shut the doors.

"I told you to stop talking to the neighbor girl. She'll never marry you. Her hand is already promised to one of the general's sons."

"Well, maybe she doesn't want to marry who her father tells her to?"

"This is the kind of stuff that gets men like you killed."

Zetetes grunts and then draws the tarp back, revealing a large stone. The sunlight beaming through the window paints the surface of the rock gray, but the sides facing away from the window shimmer in dancing patterns of blue betrayed by the lamplight. Zetetes lives on the mainland, not here in Atlantis, and when he told me of a great stone from the heavens, I knew I had to have it. I didn't expect it to be so beautiful. This meteor excites me more than anything I've brought into my workshop and most of the things I've produced here.

My admiration and awe of the meteor were cut short as Zetetes moved to pick it up. I went to help him, but he didn't need help. He held a stone larger than his torso without any grunts, shakes, or other signs of exertion. Now, I was even more intrigued.

"Where should I put this?"

I motion for him to follow me and rush to one of the workbenches. There isn't much on it, just a half-finished schematic and some scrap parts of a machine I designed to walk on its own. I swipe my arm across the workbench, and the items atop the table scatter onto the floor.

"I want to study this. I won't know what to produce

with it until I understand its properties."

Zetetes sets the meteor down. "Since I found it in that crater last week and told you about it, with how interested you were in possessing it, I took to calling it 'aletheium.' Hopefully, you can appreciate that."

I meet his eyes for a brief second before turning my attention to the meteor. "I do. I can't express how much I appreciate you bringing this to me."

"I know you're eager to work on this, and if I stay here any longer, I won't be home before nightfall."

Zetetes cranks the winch to open the door. The abundance of sunlight makes the aletheium return to a dull gray color. My cousin hoists his cart up to his waist and turns it around to face the door. He takes a few steps but pauses in the middle of the doorway. He seemed like he wanted to say something. I could feel his tension, but he sighed and walked out of the workshop without another word.

I wait a few seconds and close the door. It's time to do what I've done almost every night since my husband left me alone here. It's time to bury myself in my work.

***

Three days later, I had the forge burning with the heat of three suns. The aletheium is in my rolling crucible, essentially a large pot on a steel frame with tracks, so I don't have to hire four men to move it for me.

The first night I studied the meteor, I had a vision. I was transported out of my body, and I could look down on myself from above. I could see the workshop for the first time as an observer instead of an occupier. I floated around the city as most were sleeping. When I returned to my body, the experience lingered, and I knew what to do with the aletheium.

I push the crucible over the forge. After I lock the wheels, I take a step back to marvel at it. In mere moments, the bottom of the crucible is beginning to glow orange. I bring the step ladder over and peer inside the melting pot. The aletheium has already completely melted. A layer of black slag is floating on top of the radiant blue liquid.

I wheel the mold into place next to the forge. This process is essential. I have to be careful not to spill or waste any of the aletheium. There's no telling if there is more of it on the entire planet, given it is a rock that hurtled down from the sky. I put on the protective, thick leather apron and moved next to the crucible. I make sure everything is lined up and then slowly pull the chain dangling from the side of the contraption.

With a hiss, the glowing blue liquid streams into the opening on the top of the mold. There's a series of small cracking sounds, and I wonder if the cast will burst open at the seams, rendering this whole experiment useless. I wrap a rope around the mold, and as the cracking intensifies, I tie the rope in a loop and insert a bronze sword handle into it to create an industrial-strength tourniquet.

The plume of smoke escaping the top of the mold has subsided into a light lilting of steam, and all but the crackle of the forge coals has silenced. So long as I don't disturb the cast, I think it will be fine. What kind of an artisan would I be if I screwed up an opportunity that only comes once in an eternity? I'll finish the frame tonight, and tomorrow, I'll crack open the mold and let my creation see the world for the first time.

The next evening, I press the chisel's tip against the mold seam. The seam pops apart with a few gentle hammer taps and my heart races. The clay has become brittle, and the top of the mold falls in half as I pick it up.

After removing the other part of the mold, I lay the mirror onto a workbench. If I'm right. This mirror will show people their true selves, not just their physical appearance. It will need some polishing, but this may be the most important item I've ever produced in this workshop. My magnum opus, the aletheium mirror.

***

My vision is blurry, and it's almost dawn when I return to the Memory Room. My thoughts race between an urge to throw up and the wonder of being in Atlantis for so long. I'm drained, and I know I'll be in bed all day.

When my vision focuses, I look out the window and see Cedric standing in the field. We make eye contact, and he puts his telescopic spyglass in the inside pocket of his jacket. The Guardian stayed silent as I left the room and staggered to bed with a splitting headache. I take a few sips of water and an aspirin before I bury myself under my quilt.

Ethan McGrane

Chapter 43

Loss

Since Gerald didn't drive me this time, I was a couple minutes early to my appointment with Dr. Calloway. In my spare time, I tried to memorize her waiting room. The doctor seems to be a neat freak. I couldn't discern anything that wasn't centered or aligned with another object, and there wasn't a lick of dust to be seen. Even the trash in the waste basket between two armchairs seemed to have been staged. Three balled-up pieces of paper, nearly identical in size and color, could be seen through the walls of the wire mesh receptacle.

A few minutes passed before the door to Dr. Calloway's office opened. Out stepped a blonde woman. She looked like she was only a couple years my senior. There was an awkward tinge as my eyes met hers. Mine were likely dead in appearance. "Cold" and "uncaring" is how I am usually described. This woman quickly turned away from me as if to make me forget the redness and puffiness of her face's central features.

"You're on time today. Come on back," Dr. Calloway beckons to me.

I get up and move to the same seat I sat in during my last session.

"So, how have you been? It's been a couple of weeks."

"Oh, I've been fine. The past few days I've mostly been trying to occupy myself. Had the house to myself. It's so quiet."

"Is it an adjustment, being alone?" Dr. Calloway asks.

"No, not really. I've lived alone for pretty much all my adult life."

"You were eager to fly the nest?"

"I didn't move out on my own until my second year of college."

Dr. Calloway readjusts herself on the couch. She glances at the ceiling for a moment before looking back at me. "That doesn't seem like a good time to move."

"Things weren't the same at home after my father passed away."

"That's understandable. Many people find it's easier to deal with grief in new surroundings."

"I'm afraid I've made a habit of it."

"Why's that?" Dr. Calloway asks.

"Well, I left home after my father died, I left my hometown after my mother died, and now I live in a whole different state after my best friend passed," I explain.

"And has running away from your problems worked so far?" Dr. Calloway asks.

I'm caught off guard by her question. She was so blunt that my first instinct was to become defensive. It felt as though she was attacking me for listening to my gut. I thought she was baiting me, so I decided not to bite down on the hook and answer plainly, "No."

We both sit in silence for at least a minute. The silence remains unbroken as the doctor stands up. I wonder where she thinks she's going off to. We still have at least another half hour. She walks over to the bookshelf recessed into the wall. She peruses the books for a moment and then slides one out. She returns to the couch and then slides the book across the coffee table to me.

I pick up the book. It's a hardcover, all black except for big, bold, red letters. *Loss* by a name I can't pronounce, with a Ph.D. behind it.

"I want you to read this," She says.

I thought we were just doing show and tell, I wanted to say. But instead, I just say, "Okay," and pick up the book.

For the rest of the visit, we just made small talk, and then she ushered me back into the world it's her job to help me navigate better.

Chapter 44

A Gift

I shut my laptop. Behind it is the book Dr. Calloway gave me that, two days later, I've yet to even read the dust jacket.

Yesterday, I felt anxious. I couldn't put my finger on why I was feeling that way, so I tried meditating for the first time in years. After twenty minutes of forcing myself to sit still and ignore the world, I concluded I needed to get a sense of normalcy back in my life. After four hours of sprucing up my resume and another two hours of applying to job boards for remote-work accounting jobs, I'm ready to take a break.

I empty a can of soup into a bowl and slide it into the microwave. Three minutes should be enough. I believe in using each space for different functions. Multifunctional areas crowd the mind and decrease productivity. I set out a placemat at the head of the dining room table and put a spoon on top of it. With two minutes left on the microwave, I hear the ethereal hum of the Guardian upstairs.

What could he want? I wonder as I climb the stairs. He hasn't beckoned me to the attic during the daytime since he took issue with the roofing crew. Maybe there's a bird perched on the window of the Memory Room he wants me to shoo away.

I round the corner at the top of the stairs and text Cedric to tell him the Guardian is calling me. Before I pull the stairs down from the attic, I feel my phone vibrate with Cedric's response. He says, "I've a way to deal with the Guardian now, just say the word."

I respond, "Not yet. I'm not ready to end this."

I climb the stairs into the attic. The door to the Memory Room is already open. As soon as I step through the threshold, the almost angelic voice of the Guardian rings through the space in the middle of my brain. I swear, I'll never get used to hearing people as if they were my own thoughts.

I have something for you... a gift.

I glance around the room to see if there's anything out of place.

Not that kind of gift. I have knowledge to impart to you.

"What knowledge?" I ask.

You... I know you grieve, the Guardian says, in almost a growl. It makes the skin on the back of my neck prickle. *The locket... A previous user... they knew how to use the locket with intention. They could replay memories from their own lives... Perfect detail... They were able to spend time with their lost loved ones again.*

Once I process what the Guardian told me, I think about all the people I've lost over the years. I think of all the memories I could relive, all the good times. I could go back to when I was fourteen, and I got to spend the evening alone with my father because my mother was at the hospital with Gerald. He snapped his ankle during baseball practice, and since my dad was at work, my mother had to be the one to take him to get care. My father, acknowledging it was rare for us to spend quality time together, took me out for dinner. That may have been the only time just the two of us had dinner together. We were laughing with each other by the end of the night, and the next day, it felt like it never happened.

I could spend time with my mother again. I can have a night out on the town with Mandy again. Fond childhood memories can be retrieved and replayed with every detail.

I thank the Guardian for his revelation and tell him I'll return after sunset to try it out.

Once I'm downstairs, sufficiently safe enough to think my thoughts without Arnold Hastings intruding, I wonder if I want to open this Pandora's box. Using the locket is inherently harmful to my physical well-being. It's addictive enough seeing these lost scenes in history but to be able to relive the best parts of my life, on a whim no less, I worry about whether I'll be able to refrain from overusing the locket.

The microwave chirps to let me know I've forgotten about my meal, and I decide I have an entire afternoon and evening to worry about how I'll use the locket.

Ethan McGrane

Chapter 45

The Final Visit

I open the door for Cedric. I almost didn't recognize him in the twilight. Instead of his standard, colorful suits, he's wearing a black one, a black tie, and a deep, bloodred shirt. Sparse raindrops have marked his shoulders. He's carrying a briefcase in his left hand.

"Are you sure you are ready for this, Miss Emma?"

"I'm positive," I say before I direct him to the living room.

He sets the briefcase on the coffee table but doesn't open it. "When you go upstairs. Dial my number. If this goes wrong, it will go wrong fast, and you need to be able to signal me quickly."

"I've got it. Do you think he'll believe me?" I ask.

"If I was certain, I wouldn't have the kit with me," He gestures to the briefcase.

"I get the feeling you don't think this is the right course of action," I say.

"Personally, no. I wish you wouldn't step foot in the Memory Room again, and you would let me get rid of the

Guardian the way that Thaddeus and the Theosian Order have deemed the best manner to deal with occupation by non-corporeal beings," Cedric pauses, giving me a chance to interject, but I don't. "But I understand you want to give Arnold Hastings a chance to move on to a better afterlife. As your friend, I am respecting your decision while preparing you for the danger."

"The sun's down. Let's get this over with," I say.

Cedric takes out his cell phone and puts it on the coffee table next to his briefcase. "I'll be making preparations for the failsafe."

I turn around and exit the living room. For the second time today, I climb the stairs to reach the Memory Room. With each step, a memory of my historical endeavors flashes through my mind. I've been so preoccupied with living other people's lives that I've let my own derail.

The pattering of rain against the roof echoes through the attic. I've been living with this bomb at the top of my home for the last couple of months. I'm ready to defuse it.

I step into the Memory Room. *I'm curious to see what you will relive.*

"There's something my mother said to me right before she passed that I think I need to hear again," I say.

I sit down and activate the locket the same way I've done over a dozen times, but this time, I hold a crucial moment in my mind. I focus on what I want to see as I look into the eyes of the portrait within the locket, as if I'm telling this stranger what I want. The world shifts around me, but not as drastically as other times. There was only a brief moment of darkness, a blink of an eye between me and the last time I saw my mother.

There is something dehumanizing about someone in a hospital, as though being infirmed makes one less than oneself. That's one of the things I mulled over when my mother was on her deathbed. For my whole life, I had never heard my mother be called anything but "Maggie." Yet, during this time, everyone called her by her legal name, the one on her charts, on the bracelet around her wrist, Margaret. During my visits, a doctor or nurse never called her by what was on the cards accompanying the flowers on the table in the corner of the room.

My mother was a pillar of the community. She was always at the church, helping at the food pantry or lending an ear to someone who was struggling. After my father passed, he wasn't around to tell her not to give so much of her belongings and money away. She was so busy giving to others that my bedroom remained empty from when I moved out to when the house was sold three years later. She never found a purpose for the room.

The people close to Maggie Green told her she should get to a doctor about the shortness of breath and the pains in her chest. But, I think she stopped caring about herself after her husband of nearly forty years had passed and her only two children moved out. By the time she went to the hospital, it was too late for anything to be done about it. What could have been treated years ago left her with weeks when it was discovered.

Gerald and I were taking shifts being with my mother. He would be here during the day while he was subcontracting out work on some houses, earning a commission. I had to be at work during the day. In the late afternoon, I would visit the hospital cafeteria and spend the rest of the evening keeping my mother company and doing schoolwork toward my bachelor's in accounting.

The window drapes glowed orange behind me this evening, and the glare was making it hard for me to see what was on my laptop screen. My mother, at this point, was in a lot of pain, and the medicine they were giving her made her primarily incoherent. She spent most of the day asleep, according to Gerald. The nurses told me she was sleeping upwards of twenty hours per day.

I expected the only interruption to my schoolwork to be the occasional healthcare worker coming in to change an IV bag or record my mother's vitals. One of the wheels on a gurney being rolled through the hallway squeaked, and my mother stirred. I barely paid her any attention because she would ask me nonsensical questions. Questions such as, "Is it snowing outside?" even though it was June. I would say, "No, ma. It's not snowing." One time, she asked me if "my mother was around." I still regret telling her, "I'm not sure."

I wanted to relive this memory before I put the locket away for good after the Guardian is dealt with because of what my mother told me.

"Emmy," she says. I was too slow to answer her the first time. She hadn't looked at me yet. I wasn't sure if she even knew I was with her at that moment. "Emmy!"

"I'm here. Right here, ma."

"Emmy, I need you to do something for me."

"Anything, ma. What do you need?"

"I need you to forget about me. Go on and live your life."

"I'm not going anywhere."

"You need to," she doubles down.

"I can't. I'm not going anywhere before Gerald gets here in the morning. Don't worry."

"Emmy?"

"Yes, ma?"

"Emmy, I would rather you forget about me for the rest of your life, than spend a single moment sad I'm gone."

I didn't reply to her. I didn't know what to say. I knew she was saying goodbye, but I wasn't ready to say goodbye, even after weeks of talking to the doctors.

"Emmy, you've got to promise."

My voice breaks, and tears well in my eyes. "I promise."

The next day, I left work early because of a phone call from Gerald.

Chapter 46

Jilted Spirit

Tears stream down my face as I return to the pitch-black Memory Room. I check my phone. It's only been two hours since I entered the memory through the locket, making it one of my shorter sessions, but my head feels like it's in a vise.

That was... moving. The Guardian says to me, snapping me back to tonight's main event.

"I need to tell you something."

What do you have? I appear to have piqued his interest, or maybe he's doubting I have anything he wants to hear.

"I know who you are."

There's a pause, and for a second, I wonder if the Guardian is just going to lash out and kill me. I have to suppress the pit of fear within my stomach. *Well? I'm waiting.*

"You're the previous owner of the house. You're trapped in this room because you succumbed to the locket. You're Arnold Hastings."

A pale blue light forms in the corner of the room. It was faint at first but grew to fill the entire space.

How long have you known this?

"A couple of days. I wasn't sure how to tell you or if now was the right time."

Who was Arnold Hastings? Was he important?

I don't like how the Guardian is still speaking in the third person about Arnold Hastings. "From what I could find, you were a good man. You were a well-respected lawyer. Your daughter was married right on the lawn outside that window," I point to the circular window on the wall.

And I threw it all away because I couldn't stop myself from using the locket?

My mouth suddenly goes dry. I'm cold, colder than I was that night I was locked outside my apartment in February a few years ago.

You're lying to me.

"It's the truth. I swear."

Don't you swear to me!

I stand up, my knees are wobbling, every step is taking effort I'm unaccustomed to giving. My breath starts to catch in my throat. Every exhale rasps, and every inhale feels like sand poured into airways. I stagger, and when I reach my arm out to catch myself on the wall, it folds against me, and my shoulder slams against the wall.

The blue light filling the room glows so intensely that I close my eyes to shield them from the strain. But even through my eyelids, the light is too intense. I shuffle myself weakly against the wall, trying to find the door.

Do you think you can deceive me?

"I told you the truth!"

I don't believe you.

My hand finds the doorframe, and I clasp my hand over it, ready to stagger out of the room. Something scrapes across the left side of my forehead, and an instant later, the door slams on my hand. I cry out in pain and pull my hand back, clasping it in my other hand. The door clicks shut, and I know that I'll never be able to open it without the Guardian allowing it.

I'm in his domain now. Here, Arnold Hastings is synonymous with God. Arnold is an angry god.

Embracing the Forgotten

know that I'll never be able to open it without the Guardian allowing it.

I'm in his domain now. Here, Arnold Hastings is synonymous with God. Arnold is an angry god.

Chapter 47

Malfirothes

My hand and forehead are searing with pain.

"You broke my hand!" I grimace through grit teeth.

The blue light fades in intensity. I open my eyes but immediately have to shut my left eye because something liquid pours into it. With my right hand, I touch my forehead, and the back comes away black. I know that in the blue light, the black liquid is blood. I look down at my left hand. Blood is seeping from a cut across the back of it from where the corner of the door struck me.

My ring finger is stuck bent in half, and pointed at my wrist. The tip of my little finger is stuck propped against the middle of my ring finger. Despite my best efforts, my middle finger remains relaxed, half-curled. Moving my thumb, index finger, or wrist causes the rest of my hand to erupt in agony. I press my left arm against me as though my arm were in a sling.

I should do worse to you. You… You betrayed me.

"I told you the truth!"

You said you were going to help me.

I smell my blood as it rushes past my nose. It tickles

the skin as it flows down over my eyelid. The blood feels warm against my cheek, and there are audible tapping sounds as the first few drops hit my shirt collar.

I start to feel light-headed. The vision in my right eye starts to shimmer and fade around the edges. I brace myself against the wall. I try to steady my quick and shallow breaths while simultaneously suppressing the urge to vomit.

I close my right eye. At first, it was intended to be a blink, but it felt like my eyelid wanted to stay shut, and I didn't have the willpower to force it open. In my mind, I mull over how I'm probably thinking my last thoughts. I'm at the mercy of an angry god, and there's nothing I can do about it.

My legs start to give out from under me, but before I fall, an overwhelming force straightens my body upright, and both of my eyes are flung open, letting the blood pouring down my face into my eye.

Look at me!

In front of me, the apparition of Arnold Hastings's spirit takes shape. He looks like all those spirits I saw when I returned to my soul's origin before I incarnated as a human for the first time. But there's something off about him. No stars are floating within the blue tendrils composing his form.

Even if you were telling me the truth… What could I gain from it? How could I fix what has happened to me? White light pulses through his being in tandem with every word he speaks into my mind.

I'm so preoccupied with trying not to pass out, trying not to succumb to my pain, fear, and injuries, that I don't have much of my faculties left to deal with the Guardian and his mental onslaught. I hear banging on the door to the Memory Room. Cedric is asking if I'm alright. I try to say I need help, but my mouth cannot speak. I pull my phone out of my pocket and hit the call button on Cedric's number. Before it can connect, my phone flies from my hand through the window. It's surreal, seeing the glass shatter and then reform as though nothing happened in the first place.

My nonchalant reaction to losing my phone makes me realize how loopy I've become. Suddenly, I'm aware of how fast my heart is beating. I try to move toward the door again, but a high-pitched frequency floods my ears as I try to move forward. I pick up my right foot, but the Guardian pushes it backward when I try to move it forward. I try to force it forward, but my knee grates, and my leg strains with tension.

What I intended to be a step forward became a step backward. I try again, only to draw the same results. Arnold's spirit floats in front of me, keeping pace with me and giving me the illusion of unmoving.

Perhaps I'll try again. Your next incarnation may be more keen to help me. I'll wait a couple decades before I beckon to them. It will be a blink of an eye for me but another lifetime for you.

When the back of my leg comes into contact with the chair I've willingly sat in on so many occasions, the noise ceases, and the Guardian raises his hand. A light flashes between us, and I'm flung into the throne of my impending demise.

The locket floats off the table and hovers in front of me. With the state I'm in, using the locket will surely kill me. I'll be joining Arnold in his hell. The pain in my hand and brow means nothing anymore, not compared to what is floating in front of me. I try to close my eyes as the button on top of the locket is pressed by an invisible hand, but the same force in control of the locket now has my eyes held open.

On second thought, there are so many lives you've lived... It ends now. It concludes with the tool you created and guided through history. Your remarkable soul... caged in the Memory Room.

My lips part. Some blood drips in through the corner of my mouth. I want to ask for mercy, but I can't speak. Suddenly, the blue light cuts out. It's pitch black again. I can move on my own accord once again, but I'm too terrified to.

The door slams open, and the warm white light of the main attic space floods in as Cedric rushes into the Memory Room. I want to spring up into the arms of my savior, but my body doesn't have the energy to. Cedric puts his hand on my shoulder and shines a flashlight on me. From what I can see of his face around the edges of the flashlight glare, his eyes are wide.

"I shouldn't have let you come up here."

I close my eyes tight. Tears escape the inner corners of both of my eyes. My left hand sits motionlessly in my lap. My right hand is holding something, a small piece of jewelry.

"Can you walk?" Cedric asks me.

I open my right eye and look at him. Before I can nod affirmatively or say, "I think so," the sound of rushing air, as though we were in a wind tunnel, courses throughout the room, but it doesn't ruffle Cedric's color, and the room seems undisturbed. The darkness in the room is replaced by a crimson glow.

I assumed that Arnold Hastings had returned. He's back to finish what he started. But Cedric pulls me out of the chair by my good arm and leads me toward the door. "We need to leave now!"

"What's happening?" I ask as the house starts shaking.

"The demon I summoned, Malfirothex, he got rid of the Guardian, but he hasn't left yet."

Chapter 48
Macabre Maze

A deep, booming voice rings through the house. This voice sounds like the villain from an 80's movie, but with the rattling of a chainlink fence undercutting every word.

"Cedric Renaud. You called me, offering nothing for my services. You didn't tell me such a powerful artifact was right under my nose."

"I don't make transactional relationships with demons, Malfirothex."

"I'll make a deal with you," A pale man with no hair in an all-black suit and black, lifeless eyes appears in the corner of the attic as Cedric is helping me down the stairs to the second floor. When I make eye contact with him, he grins wickedly. "You give me the locket, and I'll consider the debt paid."

I tighten my hand around the locket. I may not be thinking clearly, but this is my last conduit to being able to spend time with my father, mother, and Mandy ever again. Cedric tells me to "just keep moving."

Malfirothex stands at the end of the hallway when I descend the stairs. He stares at me, still grinning. "You don't have to want to give me the locket. I'll get it either way. At least you've decided to resist. Now I can take the locket the fun way."

Cedric whispers into my ear, "He can't touch you. He's a non-corporeal being."

Malfirothex lets out a low, guttural laugh. "I don't need to touch her."

Cedric puts his hand on the small of my back and lightly pushes me forward. Every fiber of my body tells me not to walk toward the demon, but Cedric is behind me, telling me I'll be fine. We wouldn't be in this situation now if I had taken Cedric's advice. I continue to walk forward toward the monster who's smiling at me.

Malfirothex stretched his hands out and tilted his head, posing as though he were Jesus in a Renaissance Era painting. The locket heats up in my hand. My vision warps. The red light my house is flooded with is replaced by a kaleidoscope of colors. Instead of walking through the hallway of my second floor, I'm standing on top of the railing of the Williamsburg Bridge in New York City.

I recognize this body. I'm Amelia Evans again. I stretch out my arms as a passersby shouts, "Hey! Don't do it!" It was a combination of following through with a laid-out plan and spite for the man who was about to list reasons there might be to live for. I allow myself to fall forward. I don't scream or flail my limbs in the time it takes me to drop almost one hundred and fifty feet from the pedestrian walkway to the surface of the water.

With a sharp gasp, I'm back in my house. Malfirothex is still standing at the end of the hallway, and Cedric is holding me up. I start walking toward the demon again, but as soon as I step forward, the kaleidoscope warps reality again.

I'm standing in front of Ishtar's temple in Eridu once again. I'm in a defensive posture, my back against the door to the temple. An angry mob stands in front of me. The man at the head of the mob is holding a long dagger. I'm standing between him and the wife who's been unfaithful to him, who he intends to kill for the shame she's wrought him.

The mob asks me to step aside, but I declare I will not move. These commoners aren't allowed to harm me. To hurt a religious leader in this society is one of the greatest shames, even greater than having a wife who bedded your business rival. All the rules of this culture are swept aside by this man's anger, and he slashes his dagger across my face. The crowd's chants are silenced momentarily, but as the man stabs the blade through my sternum, the crowd once again erupts into cheers.

With another gasp, I return to my hallway. Malfirothex is now standing around the corner at the top of my stairs. He lets me take several steps this time. His body is eerily motionless, though it stays oriented for his black eyes to stare into mine.

As I round the corner, the kaleidoscope again transports me through time. Which of my antecessors will I have to relive the death of this time? I don't have to wonder for long. I'm Alessandra De Medici, staggering through the streets of Florence, highly inebriated.

As I walk along a street parallel to a canal, a stray cat darts in front of me, scaring me and causing me to lose my footing and tumble into the canal. I'm too drunk and disoriented to right myself in the water, and the garments I'm wearing are too restrictive for me to adequately maneuver. I panic as the oxygen in my blood runs out, and my brain shuts down.

The terror of drowning lingers with me as I return to my house. I want to slump to the floor and give up, but Cedric holds me up and tells me to keep going. His encouragement gives me a second wind, and I turn the corner to the stairs. Malfirothex is grinning up at me from the foyer.

I sensed Malfirothex was growing impatient as the subsequent visions flickered rapidly. The Viking Age woman, Astrid, who I admired for her strength and perseverance after her husband died, passes away from a fever, her life slowly fading before her eyes. Then Beatrice Taylor, the Victorian London maid who swiped the locket from her employer's private collection, is beaten in the street and left in the gutter to succumb to her injuries. My heart races at what feels like a thousand beats per minute as the third vision in this rapid succession materializes. I'm in a desert alone. Aya, the Ancient Egyptian Artisan, lies with her back against a rock, starving to death while on a pilgrimage.

When I return to the house, Cedric has an arm around my collar, pulling me back from falling the remaining half of the stairs. I start to cry again, but Cedric tells me to keep moving forward, that we are almost out of the house. Though the door is only ten footsteps away from me, it feels impossibly far because of the demon standing between me and it.

I get to the bottom of the stairs. Malfirothex is directly in front of me. I feel his hot breath on my face as he lets out another round of his guttural laugh. The locket sears my hand as the kaleidoscope emanates this time from within Malfirothex's eye to encapsulate my reality.

I'm standing on a large wooden platform when I become aware of my surroundings again. A crowd stretches before me, filling the streets between the gray stone buildings. At first, I think I'm some kind of speaker or celebrity. But I'm Isolde Kovacs, and my hands are tied behind my back while two large men hold me in place. A rag has been tied around my mouth, gagging me. The crowd starts to stir as a rope is placed around my neck, and the lever is pulled to drop the floor from underneath me. I cry out through the gag as I'm dangling in the space below the gallows. A little girl in the crowd's front row is making eye contact with me. With every heartbeat, the black at the edge of my vision encroached further on my life. I see two hands clasped around the little girl's shoulders, and when I look up, my eyes meet the pitch black of Malfirothex's.

The next thing I knew, I was in utter bedlam. Steel clamors around me, and the din of battle fills my ears. I taste blood, but it's not mine. Sigurd Haraldsson has found himself far from his home, fighting a war on a foreign land. The Normans, with whom we were supposed to have a treaty with, have grown tired of us and don't want us on their land anymore.

A sword crashes through the rawhide at the edge of my shield and clips my shoulder. As I'm trying to break free from the man who wounded me, another sword runs through my gut from my right side and protrudes through my left side before it is pulled back through. I grin as I realize my journey has ended, and my last breath is to spit blood into the face of the man who has ended my life.

Cold– intense, bone-chilling cold is the next thing I feel. The thin frame of Meiying sits against a wagon, huddled between her personal guards. Though in the court he had said otherwise, Emperor Jianhua covets the amulet she told him of, demanding she return to Custodius Verus's estate with a wagon full of gold and exotic East Asian goods. Meiying warned the emperor of the winter and the treacherous paths, but he did not relent. Meiying's cart got stuck in a mountain pass. The following people to find her salvaged the gold and left her and her guards' bodies in the snow.

Ancient Greek high society treated very few philosophers well. Lyra only got a taste of decadence before the poison-laced wine took effect. With his military background, Zenon would often dine with other military elites. Lyra jumped at the opportunity to attend such a feast, and Zenon was happy to oblige her. He wasn't aware of the feud and the power grab underway. Lyra died on the floor of a grand estate, stabbing pains ripping through her body while she violently vomited.

I find myself in Renaissance Italy for the second time tonight, but I'm in Venice this time. I catch strangers' gazes following me from alleyways. I've seen the same handful of people for the last couple of days. They know about the locket, and they know I have it. They burned down Master Antonio's laboratory, but it wasn't enough for them. They want something of value. I need to get home. Hopefully, I'll be safe there.

I fumble for my house key and unlock my front door. In the dim interior, a shadowy figure approaches me. I tell them to stay back as I reach for a candlestick next to the door. Before I can defend myself, the figure clasps a hand over my mouth and slits my throat with my own kitchen knife. As I'm bleeding out, gasping, and sputtering, he rifles through my satchel until he retrieves the locket.

Atlantis, the setting of my most recent historical foray, stretches before me. After the earthquakes started a few days ago, I sent all the valuable items produced in my workshop, including the mirror, to Zetetes. Crowds rush about the streets, desperate to escape the city. A retaining wall failed in the third ring, and scores of homes sank into the ocean. Since then, the earthquakes have been steady, and we expect they'll get worse. A tremor, more violent than any in the recent days, strikes. I hear the columns crack on the building next to me. When the building starts to slide into the street, I try to get out of the way, but there are too many people around me, and I'm buried in the marble and concrete. The nightmare doesn't end there, though. I'm left a broken and crumpled mess beneath the rubble. Water fills the gaps between the debris, and I'm forced to wait as it rises above my face. I'm helpless as I sink with the rest of Atlantis.

Chapter 49

Escape

Cedric shakes me back to reality. It takes a while for me to reorient myself. I have to focus on his face, on his hand around my shoulders. I focus on the floor beneath me, the wall behind me, and the red light still permeating the atmosphere. The locket still sits in my hand. Throbbing pain surrounds it. I'm tired of this game.

I try to throw the locket away, but it's stuck to my hand. I move my left hand to pluck the locket from my right, but my fingers are still twisted in odd manners, and I can't move them. Blood still seeps from the cut on the back of it.

"Just let him have the locket," I tell Cedric.

Cedric nods and moves his hands from my shoulders. He cradles my right hand in his, and with his left, he pinches the locket. There's a sickening sound as the skin peels away with the locket. Tender flesh and burnt tissue are left under it, the floral pattern of the locket's shell rended into my palm. Cedric throws the locket down the hallway, and the red light fades in unison with Malfirothex's guttural laughter. The weightless sensation, the rushing air, it's all gone.

Cedric turns on the hanging lamp in the foyer. I look

down at the scorch mark on my right hand. The white tendons are visible. My left eye has swelled, and the blood has coagulated, gluing it shut.

"We need to get you to a hospital," Cedric says.

"I need a minute," I reply. I can't get up right now, even if I wanted to. My vision fades around the corners. My eyelid feels too heavy to keep open. I relax my breathing. My heartbeat is slowing. There are no spirits or demons after me for the first time tonight. I just want to take a minute to relax. My injuries aren't going anywhere.

"Don't go to sleep," Cedric orders.

"I'm awake," I reply. A few more moments pass without me opening my eyes.

"Don't go to sleep, Miss Emma."

"I'm awake," I say again.

***

A bump in the driveway jostled me back to consciousness for a moment. At first, I thought I was in the back of an ambulance, but when I peeked my right eye open, it was too dark to be an ambulance. I was initially alarmed that I'd been abducted by a new adversary, but I saw Cedric in the driver's seat.

"Where are we going?" I tried to ask him.

"Sit tight, don't stress yourself." By his response, I wasn't sure if he had heard me or if I had even articulated my words enough for him to understand. It didn't matter because I fell asleep again shortly after he turned right at the end of my driveway onto Oak Cove Road.

***

A disinfectant alcohol wipe dragged across my right elbow's inside stirs me awake. I open my eyes and become aware of my surroundings just in time for the nurse to plunge the needle into my skin. I have to close my eyes again and turn my head away. Needles hurt exponentially less when I can't see them.

216

I open my eyes again. My left eye barely opens, but it isn't glued shut with blood anymore.

"My name is Amanda. I'm your nurse. Can you tell me your name?"

"Emma," I say. Cedric should have been able to tell them that.

"Ok, Emma. I'm in the process of putting an IV line in right now. While I do that, can you tell me what happened tonight?"

Sure. Let me start with a brief history of the world, this magical artifact humanity forgot about, the Guardian spirit protecting it, the occult order obsessed with it, and the demon they summoned to kill the Guardian. Instead of going through the trouble recounting all those details, the inevitability of them not believing me, and the possibility of them sending me to the mental ward after they patch me up, I simply say, "I don't remember."

Amanda furrows her brows as she takes the obligatory test tube full of blood and sets it aside while she connects the IV drip to my arm. "Can you tell me the last thing you remember?"

What's something innocuous I can tell them? I've been making excuses my whole life. I'm a pro by now. "I was in the attic."

"Do you remember why you were in the attic?"

"No."

Amanda picks the trash off the side of the bed and throws it into the trash can. "We had to call the police because of the nature of your injuries and arrival here. They'll be in here to talk to you in a moment. After that, Marcus from Radiology will take you to get some X-rays."

I nod, and Amanda leaves. She glances down the hallway and gestures before walking away in the opposite direction. I tried to posture myself better, ready for a large man with a buzz cut to step in and interrogate me about tonight. Is it possible to look dignified in a hospital gown, with half of my face bruised and wounded?

Instead of the hulking cop I anticipated, a petite Hispanic woman wearing a khaki-colored uniform walked into my room.

"Hey there. I'm Deputy Moreno with the Thornbrook Sheriff's Office. I have a few questions to ask you, and then I promise I'll leave you alone."

"I don't have anything better to do," I say.

"I figured. I was just trying to make you laugh. You look like you could use it. Anyway, let's start with the hard question. What's your name?"

"Emma Green."

"OK, great. Emma. You have no idea how many people get stumped on that question. Do you remember what happened to you tonight?"

"I remember going to my attic, then waking up here."

Deputy Moreno scribbles that on her notepad. "Do you know who brought you here tonight? Were you with anyone at your house?"

"No. I live alone."

She notes that. "One last question. Would you like the Thornbrook Sheriff's Department to open an investigation regarding any potential criminal activities or foul play that may have resulted in your hospitalization tonight?"

"No."

The slight pursing of her lips told me she wasn't happy with that answer. She quickly brought the smile back to her face, pulled the tri-folded piece of paper from her breast pocket, took a clipboard out of the holder on the door, and passed it to me. "Can you print your full name, address, and sign with today's date? This isn't an official statement by you. It's just to acknowledge that I've interviewed you tonight, and that you understand a report will be filed, with a corresponding number being assigned to this case. Since you verbally declined our services, the case will be closed after the report is filed, but you can petition us to reopen the case if you change your mind or remember more details from last night."

Deputy Moreno said, "Oh, never mind. I'm sorry," while I reached for the pen after she caught sight of my burned palm and saw my other hand contorted out of shape. The deputy replaced the clipboard on the door before telling me, "I hope you get better soon," and leaving.

***

The X-rays revealed a hairline fracture on my brow, as well as complete fractures of my third, fourth, and fifth metacarpal bones in my left hand. They put my hand in a splint. It extended and immobilized my wrist and all my fingers except my thumb and index finger. They told me I would need to return for a follow-up in three or four weeks.

On the second try, I was able to get through to Gerald. I wanted to keep my promise to be there for Liam's birthday, and I didn't want to return to my house yet. There are no splints for psychological trauma. Only time will heal that wound. Without getting into much detail, I talked Gerald into coming to pick me up and bringing me back down the road with him. He wasn't happy about the eight-hour round trip but agreed to it anyway.

By one in the afternoon, I was in Gerald's truck. He swung me by my house. I couldn't bring myself to go inside, so I looked for my phone in the backyard, where the Guardian flung it. Gerald grabbed my purse from the office and a shirt without blood on it for me to change into. He asked me if I wanted to pack a bag, but I told him I would be fine without one.

By some miracle, I found my phone. I couldn't get it to turn on, though. I can probably get it fixed or replaced while I'm in Groton. I get Gerald to lock the doors, then I get in his truck, and we start our little road trip.

219

Ethan McGrane

Chapter 50

The Green House

Two weeks later, I exited Gerald's truck, back at my house in Maine. I needed a suitcase to bring all my stuff back with me. The last two weeks were my closest to a vacation in a few years. It was good to spend time with the last of my family.

Gerald will spend the night on the couch to ensure I get settled in alright. I still haven't deduced whether it's for my or his peace of mind. Either way, I'm grateful for the company. The last time I was in this house, a demon was torturing me. I'll have to ask Cedric if the existence of demons means there is a Hell. The thought hadn't struck me until I told Gerald the whole story about what happened that night.

Cedric hadn't contacted me the whole time I was in Groton. I wanted to take my mind off things, so I didn't reach out to him until yesterday, letting him know I was coming back today. He told me he would swing by in the afternoon.

I was starting to feel hungry. Gerald and I were discussing dinner when we heard tires going through the gravel out front. I was already in the foyer, waiting for him to ring the doorbell.

I forced myself to smile when I opened the door. For one thing, I wanted to let him know I missed him the last two weeks and to show him I was feeling better. For the most part, my face has healed, but I have a scar splitting my left eyebrow in half. I still have the splint on my hand, which hurts quite a bit, but I don't want Cedric to worry about it.

"Miss Emma, you look good today. Much better than I saw you last."

"Thanks," I invite Cedric in. The two of us enter the living room and join Gerald in front of the dormant television.

"Hey bud, good to see you," Gerald says to Cedric.

"You as well," Cedric replies.

I didn't expect it, but silence overtook the room. Cedric was the first to break it. "So, what are your plans now?"

"I haven't thought about it," I answer.

"There are two choices," Cedric says. "You can return to your life and move on like this never happened. Or you can accept the magic in the world, both good and evil, and help us at the Theosian Order make a difference."

"You don't owe anybody anything, Emmy," Gerald chimes in.

I can almost hear Dr. Calloway telling me to stop ignoring and running away from my problems.

"You don't have long to decide. I've filed my preliminary report with the order, and once I issue my final one, they'll cut my housing and food allowance, and I'll have to return to the headquarters outside of Washington DC," Cedric says.

"What could I possibly offer the order?" I ask.

"We need people like you. We need people who don't run from the noises in their attic. We need people who, even though a spirit can kill them in an instant, will still try to help them instead of summoning a demon to divinely eviscerate them."

"A load of good it did you last time," Gerald reminds me.

I'm still curious about Cedric's offer. He's always been secretive about the order. "What would the job look like."

"It's a lot of traveling, a lot of following up on rumors, and a lot of dead ends and hoaxes," Cedric says.

"So, this," I gesture around the room, "was out of the ordinary?"

"Very much so. These types of cases are few and far between. The average Theosite may only encounter one or two of these such circumstances," Cedric says.

"So, I would get to travel the world and help people the way you helped me?"

"We mostly operate in the United States and the United Kingdom, but yes. With your permission, of course, we can use this house as a home base for our New England operations. There are four open cases in Maine, three in Vermont, and two more in New Hampshire. We tried to acquire the Oak Cove House when we discovered the locket was here, but the order didn't have the discretionary funds, and protocol dictates we can't settle in a building with pre-existing spiritual habitation," Cedric explains.

I take a moment to think about it. Aside from the risk of death and injury, I can't think of a reason to say no. "I'll join the order," I say.

Cedric grins. "I'll let my superiors know. We can call this place The Green House."

"I like the sound of that," I say.

Gerald rolls his eyes. "I'm not gonna join your ohdah, but I always say people need direction. Maybe this can be yours, Emmy."

"Maybe."

Author's Notes

The idea for this novel came to me in a dream. The dream wasn't as involved or complex as this novel turned out to be. It was me on a walkthrough of an old house with a real estate agent named Emma. During the dream, when we got to the attic, Emma told me there was a "special room up here" that allowed me to see memories from my antecessors.

Antecessor, brought down to the roots, means "one who came before." It is similar to the word *ancestor* and means the same thing without context. I use the term antecessor to refer to the person somebody was before their current incarnation. I believe in reincarnation. Many cultures throughout history have believed in reincarnation.

One of the things that makes it so intriguing, the idea of reincarnation, of antecessors, is there is usually a veil or a transformation that occurs, which makes the current incarnation forget the previous. In a past life, was I a storyteller? Maybe. Emma Green was also in the finance industry in the past, but she was also so much more: a craftsperson, artisan, and religious leader.

Emma is one of the rare souls continually recycled

throughout the history of the world. She can see all the way back to the early days, before written language, before any significant innovations, before we settled in permanent steadings. Where Emma can see all the way to humanity's infancy, someone else using the Memory Room may only see back a few thousand years, and still, another may see nothing.

There are more humans alive now than have ever lived before. Unless you want to cede that some humans have no souls, which I am not willing to say, it must stand that new souls are created every day. Emma is lucky to have a spirit containing so many stories. Her name, *E. Green*, was a play on the word *evergreen*, a reference to her soul's eternal nature.

Cedric Renaud. A man from Cameroon who developed an interest in mysticism at a young age came to travel the world searching for secrets left behind by figures such as Aleister Crowley, Jack Parsons, Anton LaVey, and H. P. Lovecraft. Cedric discovered and kept a close eye on the Oak Cove House in Maine.

The story in this novel went through several iterations, and the final product was much different than what was initially drafted. Originally, there was no Guardian. The story was straightforward– a woman buys a house and finds a magic locket inside it. She starts using the locket, and a mysterious man, Cedric Renaud, seeks to take the locket from her.

I much prefer the story as it turned out. I hope you, the reader, also found enjoyment in this story. This is my second completed work. I learned much from my first novel and applied it to this one.

When you peel away the fantastical elements of this book, take away the guardian spirits, the demons, the magic locket, and the occult societies, this book is about healing. So far, in my twenty-five years, I have never met someone who could not use healing of some form.

I maintain a website, https://mcgrane.blog. There may be supplemental materials on there, such as visualizers for some of the settings or characters, histories about certain things… etc. It's my central hub for my work. There's a tie-in short story available there: *The Triangle Pact.*

Please reach out to me. You can find me on social media (at the time of writing this, Facebook, Instagram, and X). I'm always talking about my books there, and I would love for my readers to join me. Tell me how you liked the story. Tell me your favorite scene or something that resonated with you. You can also email me, and I'll subscribe you to my newsletter, at ethanvmcgrane@gmail.com.

It would help me a lot if you leave a review on your favorite book service. I would name some, but some distributors won't like that.

Thank you for reading. It really means the world to me,

Ethan McGrane